HANNAHAN'S LODE

According to Deputy George Johnson, the three Geoghegan Brothers were planning to hit the bank in Hannahan's Lode. When they hit the Forrester Mining Company instead, its payroll goes missing and Brad Forrester is murdered. Johnson's mistake leaves him and Marshal Hills out of a job. When a replacement payroll leaves Deadwood by stagecoach, the two new, cowardly lawmen leave Johnson and Hills to try and capture the bandits. They get to the outlaws before they can reach the stagecoach — but, somehow, the payroll vanishes . . .

Books by Jim Lawless
in the Linford Western Library:

BLOODY TRAIL TO DORADO

JIM LAWLESS

HANNAHAN'S LODE

Complete and Unabridged

LINFORD
Leicester

First published in Great Britain in 2004 by
Robert Hale Limited
London

First Linford Edition
published 2005
by arrangement with
Robert Hale Limited
London

British Library CIP Data

Lawless, Jim
    Hannahan's Lode.—Large print ed.—
Linford western library
1. Western stories
2. Large type books
I. Title
823.9'14 [F]

ISBN 1–84395–773–6

Published by
F. A. Thorpe (Publishing)
Anstey, Leicestershire

Set by Words & Graphics Ltd.
Anstey, Leicestershire
Printed and bound in Great Britain by
T. J. International Ltd., Padstow, Cornwall

This book is printed on acid-free paper

1

The blued barrel of the rifle was like a rigid extension of his arm. His left hand cradled the cold steel; his right hand grasped the wooden stock as his finger curled around the trigger, and against his cheek the polished wood was smooth and cool. He closed his left eye; squinted the right; lined the front sight on the heavy door of the bank some fifty yards away across the square to his left; carefully began to squeeze.

'Bang!'

Deputy George Johnson, down on one knee at the window, said the single word softly, lifted his head and grinned. He stood up, let the net curtain fall as he stepped to one side, pulled the Winchester back off the sill and propped it against the wall.

Goddamn, but his knees were aching.

He stretched, yawned, then looked

about him guiltily. Should be ashamed of himself, yawning, after a good night's sleep and still less than an hour after a misty dawn. But the hotel room was empty. Just the bare bed, washstand with bowl and pitcher, the wooden chair he'd kicked to one side, because if he'd sat on it while he was holding that Winchester to his shoulder its rickety legs might have ruined his aim when they rode into town.

George shivered, but it was more from excitement than fear. That, and satisfaction at a job that was well done. *Almost* well done.

This time when he went to the window he looked to his right across the dusty square to the general store. From this angle he could see Marshal Frank 'Distant' Hills, sitting on the gallery's boards with his back to the wall, rifle across his thighs, safe behind the innocent stack of barrels piled high for him by the store's owner, Jed Cooper.

From that position Hills could squint

across the square, looking through chinks in the stack of barrels without being seen; could, in mere seconds, be in position to blast hell out of anybody approaching the bank and looking even a mite suspicious.

And today, that was going to happen. If George was right — and, by hell, hadn't he risked his life for nigh on a week to make damn sure he was right? — the Geoghegan Brothers would come hammering into the town of Hannahan's Lode at seven o'clock, storm into the bank while the Lode's citizens were still rubbing sleep from their eyes, and pile out with gunnysacks stuffed with the cash they knew was there until nine o'clock in the morning on the last day of every month.

Only this month, it wasn't. And nor was the owner, John Kennedy, who for the past ten years had always come in early on that one day of the month. Because, on George's say so and with the backing of the town council, Marshal Hills had arranged for Kennedy to stay away and the cash to be moved out, transported on a battered old buck-board to the Forrester Mining Company a full day early — the 29th of June — to be held there for twenty-four hours until wages and such like were paid out the next day.

The miners would get their money, bills would be paid . . .

Still no movement. And now the rising sun had poked its brilliant rim over the purple horizon away to the east behind John Kennedy's bank, its fiery ball picking dazzling highlights off Frank Hills's rifle barrel as its rays slanted over the bank's roof to cast its front wall and the whole west side of the square into deep shadow.

Damnation! George looked down at the floor, cursed the red patches dancing at the back of his eyes, then again looked sideways across the square at Hills. The marshal was up on his feet now, restless — and he was looking towards the hotel room where George was holed up. Too far away to see the

4

look in his eyes, but George knew those flinty blue eyes well, and guessed that the lawman's temper — always on a short fuse — was about to blow.

But George knew he'd got it right, knew there could be no mistake. Doggone it, hadn't he been there in the flickering firelight when Sean Geoghegan had called Padraig and Jimmy close to him and used the point of his Bowie to scrape marks in the dirt to show how the bank would be robbed. The fast ride in from the west. Jimmy to remain outside the bank with the horses while Sean and Padraig stormed in to thrust a pistol under the startled John Kennedy's chin and force him to open the safe. Then out fast and away, pushing their horses hard towards the south before following a wide loop that would take them back to their camp.

That's how it would be. That's what George had heard, and that was what he believed.

But as he looked at the restlessly prowling figure of Marshal Hills and beyond him the short stretch of Main Street that, like a midsummer water-hole, mocked him with dust and silence, George Johnson felt his confidence oozing away.

'Come on,' he whispered. 'The bank's waiting. Where the hell are you?'

2

'There for the taking,' Sean Geoghegan said. A large man and black-bearded, he was relaxed in the saddle, looking at the single, pencil-thin column of smoke that rose from the long hut that was the office of the Forrester Mining Company.

'But it had better be quick,' Padraig Geoghegan said, 'or those damn miners will tear us limb from limb.' His blue eyes were dancing, his gloved hands folded on the horn.

Young Jimmy Geoghegan laughed. He was also tall, but without the bulk of his heavier brothers. 'We've not been caught as yet,' he said, 'and with those dumb miners and their boss all looking for danger in the wrong direction we're not likely to be caught today.'

Forrester's mine was set back in the foothills some five miles to the north-west of the town of Hannahan's Lode.

7

The mine's offices, stores and sleeping quarters sprawled across a naked hollow of hard-packed earth almost a mile down from the workings, and it was on a bluff overlooking these that the Geoghegan Brothers had reined in.

The mining company was in the area of South Dakota's Black Hills where the legendary miner, after whom the town of Hannahan's Lode was named, had panned the creeks for gold some thirty years before, died penniless after ten years' backbreaking prospecting and been buried on the land he had worked.

The way it was told, the bearded man digging Hannahan's grave had hit hard rock with the blade of his shovel, caught the gleam of yellow metal in the fading evening light and made the mistake of throwing a rope hackamore on his mule and riding like a wild man into the nearby settlement with the news.

He had been shot in the back as he lifted a glass of whiskey at the crude bar in the tented saloon to celebrate his lucky strike.

In the rush that followed, a thousand men had worked themselves ragged without clawing enough gold from the earth to keep them from starving. A half-drunk wag had given the town its ironic name, and it wasn't until Brad Forrester arrived there some ten years later with the money to buy machinery and establish a professional mining operation that Hannahan's seam finally became profitable.

That profit had more than once attracted the attention of men who sought for riches without hard work, but so far those lawless guns had met with fierce and fatal retribution from the miners, or finished up dangling from a length of rope behind the town jail.

'Are they at work already?' Padraig's eyes were busy, looking for signs of movement.

Sean shook his head. He was the oldest of the three by five years, the hardest by some way, and a man who always thought before he moved. Over the past twelve months the succession of robberies that had established the Geoghegan Brothers' reputation had been meticulously planned. This, the raid on the Forrester Mining Company, was no exception.

'On a normal day, they would be,' said Jimmy. 'But it's a tradition that on pay day they sleep late. Forrester doles out the cash at eleven, they're in the mine by half past.'

'And he's in there now, counting it?'

'One man, on his own.' Sean grinned at Padraig. 'Can we handle that?'

'Sure, let's go count it for him.'

The three brothers rode a twisting route down from the top of the bluff, following a deer trail with the buildings from time to time cut off from their sight by trees. But when they reached level ground nothing had changed. The bunkhouses were silent. The sun, floating up above the high ground behind the mine workings, was gradually pulling back the shadows to flood the hollow with light.

'We'll ride the long way,' Sean said softly, 'come in from the side, then go in through the door together.'

Once down off the high bluff it was apparent that the hollow was not flat. A low ridge came between the office building on one side, the stores and bunkhouses on the other, and this had been taken into account when Sean Geoghegan planned the raid. The ridge was simply a low hump stretching across the yard, but it effectively prevented any early rising miner from looking bleary-eyed from a window and spotting the three armed riders bearing down on the office. Noise would give them away, but they rode without haste through the thin dust covering the hardpan, and hooves were naturally muffled.

The office wall furthest away from the bunkhouse was still in shadow. The lie of the land and the design of the building — set high on wooden stumps — meant that with surprise on their side they were unlikely to be seen from

11

the two windows set in that long side of the office, or from the bunkhouse.

In any case, Sean thought, the miners were asleep and the man inside the office would be busy. Counting the money. He grinned. Taking one last look at it, poor fool, although he was not himself aware of that.

He led the way, and the three men rode in close to the wall and silently dismounted between the windows. Sean looked up, put a hand over his horse's warm muzzle as it lifted its head, waited, then nodded happily. While he was thus ensuring that their arrival had not been noted, Padraig pulled two folded gunny-sacks from his saddle-bag. Now, following their older brother's lead, he and Jimmy tied their reins to one of the thick stumps supporting the building, stepped away and drew their six-guns. In single file they walked along the wall to the building's short end, went swiftly up the shaky wooden steps — and Sean drew back a leg and kicked open the door.

'Stand still!' he shouted, and thrust forward his cocked pistol. 'Not one damn move out of you — or you're a dead man.'

The room was warm and airless, thick with the smell of coal oil and cigar smoke. Unlit lanterns hung from rafters; six-foot tables lined the walls, littered with papers filmed with dust; rickety chairs were scattered about the board floor, and faded maps were tacked to the walls alongside tin-types of mining operations.

At the far end of the room — on the short wall opposite the door — a stove glowed red in one corner, an open safe stood in the other. Seated at the cleared end of one of the tables, a burly man with shirt sleeves rolled up over massive forearms was reaching into the safe for thick bundles of bills and stacking them at his elbow. From him, Sean Geoghegan's barked order brought nothing more than a slight turn of the head, a shrewd sidelong glance from dark eyes set deep under black brows.

If the abrupt entry of the Geoghegan Brothers had surprised him, he covered it well. If there was any fear within him — but, no, Sean thought, not in this man. Within this man there was intelligence and raw power, and for the first time Sean caught himself wondering and worrying about his own carefully laid plans.

'I half figured this,' Brad Forrester said, as if talking to himself, berating himself. 'That damn deputy insisted you boys had your eyes set on the bank in the Lode, and like a fool I listened to him and Hills, let them move the money out . . . '

He broke off to look intently at Sean Geoghegan, stubbed out his cigar, and flashed brilliant white teeth in a broad grin. 'But you know all about that, don't you, feller, because you fed George Johnson that story bit by bit over a couple of days, then let him ride into town all cock-a-hoop and full of his own importance.'

'He was a drifter who rode into our

camp with a willingness to listen, and you won't find an Irishman anywhere without an interesting tale to tell.'

'But it wasn't planned that way?'

'If you mean is he one of us, why no, he's not. We would have got word of our designs on the bank to town one way or another. George made it easy.'

'And official.'

Close to the door, Padraig chuckled, and Sean said, 'It's not often we have a man of the law doing our work for us.'

'So . . . now what?'

'Padraig, put up your pistol and give those two sacks to Mr Forrester.' He cast a swift glance back along the room, remembering his sudden misgivings. 'Young Jimmy, you step outside and keep watch.'

'And I'm to fill the sacks with these bundles of cash?' Forrester said, still, not moving. 'What if I refuse?'

'When I set eyes on you, I told myself I was looking at a man of rare intelligence. I'd hate for you to prove me wrong.'

'Intelligence enables a man to make decisions based on sound reasoning. If I refuse to do as you ask, shouldn't your first reaction be to wonder why?'

'Indeed it should. Let's say I've done that, and decided you're clever, but too big for your own boots. Now, put the money in the sacks.'

'Do you really believe I'd let you walk in here, take the money, and walk out?'

'Young Jimmy's been watching the place for a week. There's a pattern to your operations, regular as clockwork. The miners are roused by the cook, they eat their breakfast and go on up to the diggings. You come to this office early. When he's finished doing what he has to do with the men, your manager joins you.'

'Watching us for a week is good planning, but it doesn't include the end of the month.'

'On such days, the pattern's the same but — apart from yourself, of course — it all commences two hours later.' Sean grinned. 'You'll not keep us

16

talking that long.'

'What if — '

'Enough! Get on with it.'

'Same question: and if I don't?'

'Goddammit!' Padraig Geoghegan said softly. 'Crack your pistol across the man's skull, Sean, and we'll do it ourselves.'

'But no shot,' Forrester said, not moving his eyes from Sean, 'because that would bring some very hard men down on your necks.'

'Do it,' Sean said, 'or I might take my brother's advice.'

After the briefest of pauses — that nevertheless sent another frisson of uneasiness through Sean Geoghegan — Forrester scooped one of the bundles of notes off the table and stuffed it into a sack. Then another; and, after a brief pause to scratch his head, a third.

Padraig swore angrily. He brushed past Sean, grabbed the second sack and began scooping the money into its mouth. Sean pouched his six-gun, turned away, moved restlessly down the room. He leaned across the table to look out of one of the windows, saw their three horses patiently waiting and beyond them the sun-drenched yard and the trail winding through the trees towards the high bluff. The door creaked softly in the warm breeze. Behind him there was the rustle of the money, Padraig's agitated breathing — the thump as a packet of bills fell to the boards. When Sean turned, Padraig was bent over reaching for it, Forrester's hand had strayed towards a shovel leaning against the wall — and at that moment the door banged open.

'Three men coming!'

Jimmy stepped inside, his face animated, his eyes flashing with the light of battle. He stood to one side, held the door open with the back of the hand holding his six-gun. From halfway down the room Sean could see three men in work clothes, fifty yards away, shadows long as they crossed the low ridge that split the yard.

'Are they armed, Young Jimmy?'

'One has a shotgun. But there's no problem, we can pot them from here, easy as spitting.'

'And bring the roof down on us, is that it?' Sean shook his head, threw a questioning look at Brad Forrester.

'My foreman, Ed Dyson, with two of his men. I trust nobody, least of all the rabble I employ. Every month Dyson's presence — with back-up — ensures that the money goes to the right place, at the right time.'

'So we slipped up,' Sean said softly.

'George Johnson told you what he knew — but it wasn't enough.'

Sean nodded. 'Paddy,' he said, 'I think we've got plenty in that one sack.'

'Goddammit, we've got no more than half — !'

'Leave it!'

Padraig swore softly. 'Is it the window, then?'

'We've no choice. Young Jimmy, shut that door, there's a lad.'

The door banged. Jimmy came down

the room. He skipped past Sean, took a wide swing with his pistol and cracked it across Forrester's cheek as the big man came to his feet and made a second lunge for the shovel. The mine owner went down like a log, a chair splintering under his weight. From his dark hair a worm of blood trickled into the dust.

Padraig swung the heavy sack onto the table, leaned over to slip the catch and push against the window — and shook his head.

'Damn things're jammed tight.'

Sean stepped over Forrester's inert body and grabbed the shovel. He lifted it, drew it back to rest on his shoulder — and paused.

The three Geoghegan Brothers held their breath. In the thick silence, the unconscious Forrester's breathing was slow and laboured. And through the thin door they could already hear the murmur of voices as the three men steadily approached; a sudden hard laugh; the stamp and scrape of heavy boots.

20

'If we can hear them . . . ' Jimmy Geoghegan said, grinning.

'They'll hear us,' Sean finished, and with a broad wink he swung the shovel at the window. Glass shattered, tinkling outwards in a glittering shower onto the hard ground. A horse squealed shrilly.

'Out with you, Young Jimmy.'

But Jimmy Geoghegan had already pouched his pistol and was up on the table. He ducked low, kicked at some lingering shards of glass then put a hand on the frame and leaped through the shattered window in a fearless vault into the void. Padraig craned forward to peer out, then tossed the heavy sack after his young brother and sprang onto the table. He had a cautious boot on the sill and was precariously balanced when they heard the hammer of boots on the steps, a tremendous bang from the end of the room, and the door splintered.

'Go, Padraig!' Sean said.

Out of the corner of his eye he saw his brother hesitate, then drop from the window. From the shattered door there was a roar of anger. A tall, rawboned man was already inside. His blunt hands held a shotgun. As two men crowded in behind him, he cocked the scatter-gun. Angry black eyes were taking in the scene: the shattered window, glass littering the table, Forrester down and bleeding among the remaining packets of money, Sean Geoghegan caught flat-footed.

The shotgun blasted.

Sean Geoghegan dropped flat.

He moved in the instant before Ed Dyson pulled the trigger. Hot lead hissed through the space where he had been standing, peppered the end wall. He heard Dyson roar, 'Round the side, there's others getting away,' then Sean ducked under the table. Leg muscles creaking, he came up with it on his shoulders. He grunted, heaved it towards Dyson, heard the second barrel blast and the lead hit the table-top like a handful of gravel hurled by a giant fist. Then he had spun away, and was through the window in a flat dive.

It was like swooping off the edge of a cliff. In dazzling sunlight dark shapes flashed before his eyes as he floated weightless. Then he hit the ground hard on a carpet of broken glass, felt the burn of sliced skin, the wetness of blood. Around him, razor-sharp hooves flashed as Jimmy and Padraig fought to untie reins stretched taut by the panicked horses. Amid the chaotic mass of struggling men and horseflesh, Sean rolled, came awkwardly to his feet and flashed a glance back towards the end of the building.

Already the two miners were down the steps and coming around the corner. Cold steel glittered in the sunlight. Then flame spat. A slug whined.

Deliberately falling sideways against the building as a second slug whistled close, Sean drew his six-gun and blasted three fast shots. He saw one of the men go down, roaring in pain. Then a horse wheeled close. Another shot cracked above him as Jimmy let loose from the saddle. The second man yelled, and ducked back.

'Move yourself, Sean!'

Padraig was in the saddle, the heavy gunny-sack dangling from his hand, looking anxiously towards his brother as his horse backed and wheeled. Jimmy had untied Sean's horse, and hung on to it. Now, still close, he leaned down to hand the reins to his brother. Sean grabbed them, clutched at the horn with the same hand and poked a toe at a stirrup. As he did so, from the shattered window above him the shotgun roared.

Hot blood splashed Sean's face as buckshot tore into the horse's neck. Its forelegs buckled. It went down, snorting, bubbling, and rolled heavily towards him. Desperately, Sean leaped backwards. The heavy body hit his thigh, came down on his foot. As his ankle twisted agonizingly, he pulled himself free, saw Jimmy wheel his mount, snatch at his pistol and blast a wild shot at the window.

Then the youngster again rode close. He reached down, grasped Sean's reaching hand and swung his brother up behind him. And, as enraged yells broke out across the yard, and men came bursting from the bunkhouse doors, the three Geoghegan Brothers hammered away from the Forrester Mining Company and sent their horses tearing towards the twisting trail that led to the high, sun-drenched bluff.

3

Sitting like a fat black toad behind the big desk, Councillor Sidney Tweddle was livid. His serge suit was too tight and his stiff collar was cutting into his neck, the room above Hannahan's Lode's newspaper office was small and dusty and sweltering with too many men packed into the twelve-by-twelve space, the hot air pulsed with tension, anger and frustration, and it was time for his usual mid-morning glass of cold beer that Coggins would even now be placing carefully on the polished top of Clancy's bar.

Watching the angry leader of the town council, George Johnson decided miserably that what had happened that morning was a mess of good news and bad news. It was trouble for him. It was trouble for Marshal Frank Hills, whose lean frame was deceptively relaxed as his blue eyes drilled coldly into him from across the room. And, hellfire, it sure was a heap of trouble for the Forrester Mining Company. But for Yancey Flint, it was a gift from the Gods. The dark, moustachioed man who for years had aspired to the job of town marshal was perched smugly with one haunch on the corner of the desk and twin, ivory-handled six-guns jutting from his hips and, unless George was badly mistaken, he was about to get a badge pinned on his vest. The deputy's badge would surely go to his bone-thin, ragged-haired crony, Buck Owen, who wore an inane, gap-toothed grin as he lounged against the wall by the window.

And that, George concluded, planted him and Distant firmly on the town's rubbish heap — and it was all his fault.

'I allowed you to give me nothing but the bare bones, Dyson,' Tweddle said now to the man standing before the desk, 'but even those point a damning finger at the men appointed to keep the peace and protect our property.' He turned a watery eye on Hills, ignored George Johnson and, to Dyson, said, 'Brad Forrester is dead, you say, and the money transported from John Kennedy's bank all gone — every cent. So, now that we're all assembled, put some meat on those bones. Go into details.'

Tall, rawboned Ed Dyson had brought the mining company's buckboard rattling down Main Street five minutes after Frank Hills had called George down from the hotel room and the two men were talking outside the bank. Dyson had ignored both lawmen, pulled to a skidding halt that raised a cloud of dust in front of the premises of Hannahan's Lode's weekly newspaper, *The Banner*, and pounded up the stairs to the town council's office. When a breathless Frank Hills arrived hard on his heels, he had been spilling his story to Tweddle. At sight of the steely-eyed lawman, Dyson had clammed up, and Tweddle would allow no further discussion until Yancey Flint and Buck Owen had been summoned.

'It was the Geoghegan Brothers,' Dyson said, stepping back from the desk and running fingers through his thick dark hair. 'When Hills and Johnson were stuck here like a couple of fools waiting for a bank raid that never happened, Sean Geoghegan and his brothers rode down from the hills and bust into Forrester's office at the mine. They murdered him in cold blood.'

'That makes a first,' Hills said. 'The Geoghegans are proud of their record: in four robberies spread over a year they've not taken a single life.'

'Today makes it five,' Tweddle said. 'And now a fine man's dead.'

'Why would they do that?' Hills said.

'He wasn't fast enough with the money,' Dyson said, 'so they knocked him to the floor, shot him twice in the back of the head.'

Hills shook his head. 'Doesn't make sense.' He looked speculatively at Dyson. 'And where were you? The way I heard, when Forrester was handling payroll cash, it was your job to stand guard.'

'Yeah,' Dyson said, sneering, 'and the way I heard, we had a marshal and a deputy got paid to keep this part of South Dakota clear of bank robbers and such like.'

'I can assure you,' Yancey Flint said smugly, 'the Geoghegan Brothers will be brought to trial, and hanged.'

'*You* can assure him?' Hills glared at Flint, then switched his gaze to Councillor Tweddle, sitting back now and absently drumming his fingers on the desk. 'Since when has Flint had a say in what I do?'

It was Buck Owen who answered. 'From the day you proved to every damn one of us that for five years the wrong man has been wearin' the badge,' he said, still grinning — and George Johnson exploded.

'Doggone it, Owen, are you suggesting you and Yancey Flint can do better? Is that what this is about? Have you three been conspiring while me and

Distant have been hunkered down out there for nigh on three hours — '

'Wasting time,' Owen said.

'Acting on information!' George yelled.

'Sean Geoghegan used you.'

'No!' George roared. 'I watched them, listened to them, for six days and nights. The bank was the target, they had it planned to the last detail — '

'So why tell you?' Yancey Flint was off the desk, standing with legs spread and chest puffed out. 'Didn't it strike you as odd that three bandits would spill those plans to a stranger?'

'No, because I fed them a story,' George said. 'I told them I was an outlaw, heading west to Hole in the Wall. They were impressed, asked me to join them, they — '

'Hah!' Flint was triumphant. 'The Geoghegans are a clan, they'd never bring in an outsider; you swallowed that bull, you're a bigger fool — '

'Enough!' Sidney Tweddle's plump hand slammed down on the desk. His face was red, the angry glare directed not at Yancey Flint, but at George Johnson. 'Flint's right. You were taken in. We knew something was afoot when the Geoghegans were sighted in the foothills, but I always believed that insinuating yourself into the confidence of three outlaws was at best a bad idea, at worst extremely risky.'

'Less charitable folk,' Frank Hills said, 'would call that convenient hind-sight,' and Tweddle's eyes narrowed.

'I kept my views to myself because I had confidence in the officers elected by the council to keep the peace. The council trusted you. It seems their confidence was misplaced.'

'Which leaves us where?' said Yancey Flint.

'With but one choice,' Tweddle said. He looked at Hills and Johnson and said, 'I'm removing you both from office, with immediate effect. I have no power to appoint new officers but, when my recommendation is heard by the council, the swearing in of Yancey

Flint and Buck Owen as marshal and deputy will be a formality.'

'Jesus Christ!' Hills breathed. 'You sit here pontificating about recommendations and formalities and misplaced confidence when a payroll's missing, a man's dead, and three outlaws are out there laughing — '

'Your badge, Hills.'

'Yancey Flint's a pompous ass, Buck Owen is — '

'Put your badge on the desk, and get out.'

As Hills's jaw muscles bulged and his fists clenched, George Johnson stepped forward. One hand clamped on Hill's arm. With the other he unpinned his badge and sent it clinking onto the desk. Still holding his partner's arm, he waited.

Hills took a breath. He shook off George's restraining hand, unpinned his own badge, but instead of placing it on the desk he tossed it to Yancey Flint. The big man's hand came up. Before the glittering badge had spun across the short space between them and slapped into his palm, Frank Hills had stabbed a hand to his holster and made a draw like greased lightning. When Flint caught the badge, he found himself looking into the muzzle of a cocked six-gun.

George Johnson laughed softly.

'And that,' Hills said, 'is what I call an example of misplaced confidence,' and with a cynical glance at Sidney Tweddle he pouched his six-gun and led George Johnson past Ed Dyson and out of the office.

★ ★ ★

It took Frank Hills ten minutes to clear out his desk at the jail. George Johnson didn't have one, so he crossed the street to Clancy's and ordered two beers. Sidney Tweddle arrived before Hills, collected the beer Coggins had poured for him, and took it over to a window table. When Hills came in, he joined George at the bar, deliberately turning his back on the fat councillor who had taken away his livelihood.

'With us out, next move is for Yancey Flint to raise a posse,' George said. 'Think he'll do it?'

'I put that question to him when he was trying out his feet on my desk. He told me it was no longer my concern.'

'Meaning he doesn't know?'

'Flint wants the shiny badge, not the job.'

'In the meantime, Forrester's dead, and the Geoghegans are on the loose.'

For a while there was silence. George could imagine Hills's feelings. The man had been marshal for five years, swiftly cut the level of violence from the tough miners and other rowdy elements in Hannahan's Lode so that the town was a safe place to live, and by his mere imposing presence had kept the more notorious owlhoots out in the hills where they could do little harm.

But his brusque manner did not go down well with those councillors like Sidney Tweddle. They quickly discovered that they'd hired a maverick who politely listened to orders, then ignored them and ran the town his way, and it soon became a bizarre contest between one or two officials waiting for him to step so badly out of line that his job was at risk, and a town marshal who was good at his job and admired and trusted by the Lode's citizens.

Now this. Acting on George's information, they'd staked out the bank and spent hours watching the sun come up while, five miles away, the Geoghegan Brothers had brutally shot a man dead and stolen a payroll. It had been George's idea to get close to the brothers when they'd been seen in the foothills, his gullibility that had ended with Yancey Flint and Buck Owen wearing badges.

'They must have seen me, in town,' he mused into his beer. 'Those Geoghegans. Seen me wearing a badge — and I grew me four-days' whiskers and rolled in the dust, then rode into their camp and like a fool played the rough, tough owlhoot.'

'You finished?'

'Face it, Distant, we're both finished.'

Hills shook his head. 'Who's the man who knows where the Geoghegans have been hanging out?'

'Well, I do — but by now they'll have moved on.'

'It's somewhere to start.'

'So tell Yancey Flint, let him chase shadows.'

'Flint wearing a badge doesn't stop me doing my job.'

George sipped his beer, and looked sideways at Hills. His tall, lean partner had turned around and was giving Sid Tweddle the full benefit of his steely gaze. The councillor was fidgeting, and sweating. He drained his glass, slammed it down, and hurriedly waddled out of the saloon.

'He's flustered,' Hills said. 'He spoke of formality, but I wonder if his cronies will go along with his decision to appoint Flint and Owen? And if they do, will they abide by their decision when they realize they've roped a couple of lame steers?'

'You want your job back.'

'Don't you?'

'Sure I do,' George said. 'And I can see where this is leading.'

'And why?'

'You never did listen to town councillors; I can't see you commencing now.'

'That's one good reason.' Hills shook his head. 'We'll get our badges back, but it'll take hard work, hard riding. Someone's making a fool of us, and it's not just those damn Geoghegans pulling the wool over your innocent peepers. This robbery stinks, and I aim to find out why.'

4

The thin smoke from the camp-fire they had built in a small circle of stones swirled in the warm breeze, carrying with it into the grey canopy of willows the aroma of frying bacon and beans and fresh-brewed coffee. A horse snorted down by the river, its hooves crunching in the wet gravel as it moved into the shallows. Another moved off into the deeper grass beyond the stand of trees, its coat glossy in the bright sunlight as it lowered its head to graze.

'Three thousand,' Sean said, looking up. He was sitting cross-legged by the fire, the gunny-sack in his lap.

'About half of what we expected, but not bad for a morning's work.'

'Work, you call it?' Sean grinned at Padraig, folded the mouth of the gunny-sack, tossed it onto the saddles, saddle-bags and rifles heaped further back under the trees. 'Tell that to the farmer out there walking the whole long day behind his plough.'

'Or those with picks and shovels in Forrester's mine,' said Jimmy, 'and them getting no pay at the end of it.'

'Ah, but now you're making me feel guilty,' Sean said and, as he put a hand to his heart and a doleful expression crossed his bearded countenance, both his brothers roared with laughter.

'Does this mean we're through, then,' Padraig said, choking. 'That fine plan you devised was all for nothing, and we resign ourselves to repentance, and the priesthood?'

'When you put it in those sombre terms,' Sean said, 'it's amazing how quickly guilt passes — or perhaps it was your reminder of my ingenuity that did the trick. For the first phase went remarkably well, considering and, if I say so myself, the second will surely be a masterstroke.'

Jimmy drank the last of his coffee, then gathered together the empty plates and took them down to the river. Padraig, legs stretched out and his back against the slim bole of a willow, pulled a blackened corncob pipe from his pocket and began to fill it with golden tobacco from a soft leather pouch.

Sean poured fresh coffee into a tin cup, sipped thoughtfully as he looked down the sloping bank to where his younger brother was squatting at the water's edge to scour the wetted plates with fine sand. As the blue smoke from Padraig's pipe drifted flatly to be carried into the trees by the heat of the fire, he said softly, 'A masterstroke indeed, but even the best laid plans can be ruined by a stroke of bad luck — don't you agree?'

'I do. And we both know what happened. So let's talk it through, Sean, and pick holes in it as the need arises.'

'The idea,' Sean said, 'was to let it be known that we would hit the bank in Hannahan's Lode, and when the good citizens were guarding against that, we'd go for Forrester's mine. Then, a few days later when the time was again ripe and while they were still reeling from that blow — and fully occupied elsewhere — we'd do what we'd promised, and hit the bank.'

'Just the two of us,' Padraig said. 'We anticipated a posse after the first raid. It would be led by both those lawmen, and Young Jimmy had volunteered to lead it a merry dance so our second raid would meet with no opposition in the town.'

'Run them ragged,' Jimmy said, back from the river with his eyes sparkling. 'I'd lead them halfway across South Dakota, giving them the occasional glimpse of my back to keep them amused. You two would be in Hannahan's Lode making a sizeable withdrawal from the bank.' He sent the tin plates clattering into the trees, and stood with hands on lean hips, head canted as he looked questioningly at Sean. 'But now, you don't think there'll be a posse?'

'For the moment, let's forget a possible pursuit and look at the stroke of bad luck that has maybe wrecked our plans. That was the arrival of Ed Dyson, and our hasty departure that saw us leave behind half the payroll.'

'But the aim was to take two of the mine's payrolls in the space of a few days. If we get away with just half of the first, is that so bad? Lightning never strikes twice in the same place, so the second raid should run smooth as silk through a loom.'

'To give us a chance at the second — for there even to be the possibility of a second in such a short time,' Padraig said, 'we needed to take all the first. Half might not do.'

Sean picked up a blackened stick, poked at one of the white stones surrounding the glowing embers. 'It was necessary to take the full payroll today, Young Jimmy, to force Forrester to send to the bank at Deadwood for more cash to pay his men. He would have to do that, or have a riot on his hands and no work done for a month. That replacement cash would be in

Kennedy's bank in the Lode within a couple of days, and we would strike as planned. But Forrester still has half his payroll. My concern is that he will sweet talk his miners into accepting half pay for this one month. If he does that, he'll have no need for more money until the end of next month — and we're scuppered.'

'Give them a couple of days,' Padraig said to Jimmy, 'we'd catch them with their pants down for a second time. Give them thirty, we'll ride to our deaths. That, or start killing innocent people, and so far that's something we've managed to avoid.'

'Praise be to God.'

For a while, after Sean's fervent thanks, there was a thoughtful silence broken only by the faint crackle and hiss of the fire.

'What beats me,' Jimmy Geoghegan said at last, 'is that it's not yet midday and the both of you are sitting there and already the sun's frying your brains.'

'Meaning I've been talking non-sense?' Sean looked at Padraig. 'So what d'you reckon, Paddy? We dump the young whippersnapper in the river for his cheek?'

Padraig took his pipe from his mouth, and grinned. 'Let's hear him out,' he said. 'If he can't back up his words, he gets a ducking.'

'Thanks, is more like it,' Jimmy said. He dragged one of the saddles close to the fire, sat on it, and said, 'You were both in the office with Forrester when that big bastard came through the door with his shotgun. I was climbing on my horse when the other two came round the corner with guns blazing. Now, from what you saw, would you say those men — who fought like tigers for that money — are going to settle for half pay?'

'I'm concerned that they might.'

'In their position — would you?'

'Put like that,' Sean said, 'and after some consideration, I'll admit it's unlikely.'

'So us making off with half the payroll has made no difference to your plan. Forrester must pay his men in full, so he *will* send for more cash.'

'He will.'

'And how will it come from Deadwood?'

Sean frowned. 'Gold shipments are moved by special wagon, four men riding shotgun. With one robbery already, will Forrester not consider that the better option.'

'Too obvious. A wagon under heavy guard between Deadwood and the Lode would mean just one thing. But who will know there's a payroll on the stage — except us?'

Smoke trickled from Padraig's lips and he narrowed his eyes and lifted his head to look across the smouldering fire at the sunlight sparkling on the river. Sean was drawing on one of the stones with the blackened tip of his stick. He let the silence drag on while the others waited. Then the faintest of smiles curled his lips. He nodded slowly, and looked directly at Jimmy.

'So what the hell are we doing robbing the bank, is that what you're saying?'

Jimmy, eyes crinkled with amusement, said nothing.

'He's right, you know,' Sean said after a moment. 'Some plans are jinxed from the start — or maybe not given enough thought. And bad luck is not lightning; if it strikes once, it can become a nasty habit. Out there at the mine we lost a horse, and got away by the skin of our teeth. With just two horses between us we've already got troubles. If things go wrong in town it could be a lot worse.'

'So we sit tight,' Padraig said, 'and wait for the stage.'

'Instead of us going into town after the money,' Jimmy said, 'they bring it to us.'

'Jesus!' Sean Geoghegan said, 'why didn't I think of that?'

'Because the sun's frying your brains, old man,' Jimmy said, and flung himself sideways away from the fire as both his older brothers pounced. The tussle was violent but short, the crunch of gravel and the splash of the body landing flat in the river startlingly loud, and as spray rose sparkling in the sunlight a bird flapped squawking from the willows, soared high above the Geoghegan Brothers' campsite and flew lazily away to the south.

* * *

Ten miles away, Ed Dyson looked up idly to watch the circling bird as he stood, tall and lean, hat in hand, outside Brad Forrester's house. He'd walked the half-mile through the woods from the mine office, knocked once, and stepped back from the shade into hot sunlight. Now he waited. But it was a patient wait, the wait of a man who had seen an opportunity, snatched at the moment and was now anticipating rich and pleasant pickings with little or no risk.

48

When the door was opened by a young woman with corn-coloured hair and a riding outfit of cotton blouse, tan trousers and tooled boots that gave her height and showed off her slim figure, Dyson ignored the attractive picture that had the power to tighten his throat, and looked directly into her blue eyes. He noted brief shock; the instant, intelligent awareness of what must have happened and its implications; the veil that came down to hide those inner-most thoughts that he knew full well could be more mercenary and merciless than his own.

'I heard shots. And now you're here. Is he . . . is he dead?'

Dyson nodded. 'There was a raid. The Geoghegans.'

'They took the money?'

'Some.'

'How much?'

'Maybe half the payroll.'

'What about the rest?'

There was no expression in Dyson's black eyes. 'It's safe.'

Gerry Forrester wet her lips. 'And it was the Geoghegans shot Brad?'

'I thought it was the money interested you?'

For an instant she hesitated, staring at him, trying to read his mind. Then she said, 'You'd better come in.'

The big room was cool, furnished sparsely but well, with a big window overlooking the sunlit clearing. Gerry Forrester poured two drinks in crystal glasses, handed one to the foreman. He sipped, looking at her over the glass's rim, watched her avert her eyes and move restlessly away towards the window.

He thought she was the most beautiful woman he had ever seen, but that was just her looks, the outward appearance that was always likely to deceive: he was of the opinion that her mind was devious in the extreme. Under the suspicious gaze of Brad Forrester they had, perhaps without consciously admitting it, been waiting for this moment for a long time — as far as Gerry was concerned, from the moment she married the ambitious mining man and realized it was a mistake. She craved freedom. They both lusted after money. And now they were on their way.

But all the risks were his. Gerry Forrester was locked in marriage to a man she detested, but who provided her with money and security. During the times when Forrester was at the mine and Dyson had been busy in the office, she had let him know exactly what she wanted, but had refused to do anything that would jeopardize her comfortable position. Instead, her soft lips and lustful gaze had tempted the big foreman: Dyson became her tool, the means to an end. Now, twice in two days, he had stepped over the thin line between good and bad, between the law-abiding and the lawless. He had done it for the money, of that he was certain — but had he also done it for this woman who, he sensed, could never be trusted?

She turned to face him, the sunlight slanting through the window to highlight her golden hair. 'Spell it out to me, Ed.'

'I've already been to town. Frank Hills and George Johnson have been replaced by Flint and Owen. They — and everybody else — know that it was the Geoghegans shot Brad and stole the payroll.'

'All of it?'

He grinned. 'Yeah, every last cent.'

She nodded, mentally calculating, her eyes glowing. 'And now?'

'Well, we both know Brad ran a one-man show at this end, but we also know his brother Harold over in New York is financial backer and silent partner. That means you don't inherit.'

'Harold hates me. I've always known that, never wanted the damn mine anyway.'

'Right. But the interesting bit is, with one of the partners suddenly dead, the Forrester Mining Company is still operational, I'm still foreman, and

Harold Forrester will rely on me. That buys us time.'

'To do what?'

'I've already wired him, let him know what's happened. He's a tightwad and a fast thinker. He'll want the mine to keep working, and he'll know the miners won't work without pay. He'll authorize me to get more cash sent in from Deadwood.'

'And?'

'And it won't get here.'

'Why not?'

'Because there'll be an armed hold-up, by the Geoghegans.'

She nodded, the glass clasped in both hands as she lifted it to her lips. She drank, nodded again. 'Of course there will. Everybody will be expecting that. But won't that make it terribly risky — for the Geoghegans?'

'Didn't I just tell you Hills and Johnson have been replaced by two incompetent fools?'

'Ah.' She smiled, finished off the whiskey, placed the glass on the table and came over to him. She slid her hands up his chest, placed them lightly on his shoulders. 'How long?'

'Harold will reply today. I've anticipated his response, and spoken to Kennedy at the bank. He could have arranged a special wagon and escort, but he feels it's safer to bring the cash in on the next stage.'

'A couple of days, and we'll be rich, and out of here,' she said softly, 'and all because of those wonderful Geoghegan Brothers,' and, as she lifted her hands, pulled Dyson's face down to her and kissed him full on the lips, her open eyes were distant and unreadable.

5

The heat hit them like an iron fist when they left Clancy's and walked down the street towards the jail. Out in front of the general store, burly Jed Cooper was banging and cursing as he moved the pile of barrels, casting a black look across the street as he saw Hills and Johnson emerge. Wagons trundled down Main Street. Dust spurted from deep ruts to drift in dun clouds and coat the bare, warping timber of buildings that had never seen a lick of paint.

George coughed, spat, and cast a dour glance at Frank Hills's back. This was Distant's idea, and George didn't entirely go along with it, but he was still smarting from the disaster that was the result of his undercover work, and disinclined to argue. Besides, Distant had a point. He'd made his snap decision as they came out through

Clancy's swing doors, George wiping his mouth with the back of his hand, and saw Eli Simms heading away from the jail on the way back to his telegraph office. If the old man had delivered a wire, there was a fair chance the contents had something to do with the robbery out at Forrester's. And if it didn't, well, even George was interested in seeing what kind of a mess Yancey Flint was making of his first day as town marshal.

'Everything under control, Yancey?' Hills said as he went in through the open door and looked with amusement at the new marshal with his fancy boots up on the desk and the stub of a fat cigar smouldering between his fingers. 'Sid Tweddle not working you too hard?'

'Hah!' Flint said. 'I always believed you and Johnson made out this job was pure hell so you could get the town's sympathy and justify your wages. Now I'm in here, I *know* it.'

'Meaning you've got the Forrester

robbery all wrapped up, culprits appre-hended, money back where it belongs?'

'You could say that.'

'I just did — but I'd like to hear it from you.'

'He's stalling,' George said scath-ingly. 'Feller walked in and put his boots up on your desk, had 'em there for nigh on two hours trying to figure out his next move. A posse, to chase after those Geoghegans? Hell, he wouldn't know how to swear them in, and if he did he'd have 'em running round in circles chasing their own tails.'

Buck Owen came through from the cells, saw the newcomers, and grinned.

'Thought you two'd be out lookin' for work. If it's any help, Coggins needs a swamper over at Clancy's, and there's always stalls to be cleaned out over at Wright's Livery.'

George shook his head. 'Not quali-fied. As lawmen, all me and Distant are accustomed to is collecting fines and dues and rounding up stray dogs — but we'll put your names forward in case that kind of work gets too much for you.'

'More important things to do,' Yancey Flint said and, without moving too many muscles, he flicked a slip of yellow paper towards the edge of the desk.

Watched by all three men, Frank Hills took a pair of spectacles from his vest pocket, perched them on the end of his nose and swiftly read the telegram.

'Harold Forrester, in New York?'

'Brad's brother, and the Forrester Mining Company's financial backer.'

'Has John Kennedy seen this?'

'Doesn't need to. Ed Dyson went to the bank and spoke to him straight after leaving Tweddle's office. Anticipated this feller's wire, so everything's been arranged, replacement payroll's coming in on the next stage.'

'And the Geoghegans will know that?'

'Not from old Eli Simms, they won't, but they'll have worked it out, I guess.'

'So this important thing you've got to

do,' George said, 'is to put yourself in a handy position so that, when Sean and his brothers come bustin' out of the scrub to hold up the stage, you can leap out and scare them to death with those fancy pistols?'

'They won't go for the stage: they'll hit the bank.'

'The bank!' Frank Hills was flabbergasted.

'Ain't you figured it yet?' Flint said, grinding out his cigar then leaning back with a smug expression. 'They fed that pal of yours some nonsense about hitting the bank, then went for the mine, the idea being that when we're out investigating that and maybe chasing through the scrub thinking we're hot on their tails, they'll go for the bank. Only we won't be. Out investigating, that is, chasing up empty box canyons. And, no, there's no call for a posse because, when they do hit, we'll be here waiting with the bank staked out.'

'Oh, my,' Hills said softly. 'Hasn't it

occurred to you that's what they want you to think?'

'Nope. That Sean Geoghegan, he's predictable. He comes up with a plan, he sticks to it. Tell 'em it's the bank, then hit the mine; when they're out chasing shadows, hit the bank.'

'He also avoids bloodshed. This time they killed a man. Out of character, and unpredictable. Doesn't that bother you?'

'Forrester was a tough customer, that's all. In their line of work it had to happen some time.'

Flint shrugged. He looked across at his deputy and said, 'Take that wire over to the bank, give it to Kennedy so he's got Forrester's written authority. And tell him I'll be over shortly to work out some details.'

'Like how to defend the bank against an attack that won't come?' George Johnson said, as Buck Owen picked up his hat and went out.

'That's been done once,' Flint said, 'and it cost you your jobs.'

'I think you're being outsmarted,' Hills said.

'No sir,' Flint said. 'Those Geoghegans used George; they don't know you've been replaced, and they'll figure you and him are flappin' around like headless chickens trying to undo the damage. That means apprehending the robbers. You can't do that sitting on your backsides in town, and if you're out of town, the bank's a sitting duck.'

'Talking of sitting ducks,' George Johnson said, turning towards the door, 'I ain't seen you move since you took root in this office.'

★   ★   ★

After a brief, greasy midday meal taken in the Lode's only café — a shack owned by Jed Cooper's wife and tacked on to the side of his general store — it took Johnson and Hills an easy hour's riding to reach the Forrester Mining Company. Before they set out, Hills suggested they might be out for some

61

time, and they put enough supplies for several days in their saddle-bags. Along the way they ruminated out loud and with shared bitterness and frustration at their abrupt dismissal and Tweddle's appointment of Flint and Owen as marshal and deputy, and the general lackadaisical approach the two new lawmen were bringing to their job.

'If those Geoghegans managed to fool you, George, when you were diligently carrying out your duties — at considerable risk of getting your hide punctured — can you imagine what a fine time they'll have playing with those two fools?'

'Already doing that, without losing too much sweat,' George said. 'Planted a story and carried out the first phase to stamp it as gospel; Flint thinks they'll follow it through and stick to it the way the Atchison Topeka sticks to the rails, and he's planning accordingly. Feller can't seem to see how crafty beggars like those Irish rapscallions'll always be one step ahead of him, thinking his thoughts before he does so hisself.'

'What was that word, George?'

George grinned. 'Rapscallions. As in rascals. And that's mostly what they were, before they murdered Forrester. Now ... ' He shook his head, and squinted ahead through the heat haze to the hollow with its dusty buildings that could be seen beyond the steep flank of the tree-rimmed bluff.

'Doesn't make sense,' Hills said, nodding. 'And, nine times out of ten in my experience, something that doesn't make sense usually ends up being explained contrariwise.'

'Dammit,' George said, 'that's a worse word than rapscallion.'

'Made it up,' Hills said, and touched his horse with his heels. 'Come on, let's see what Ed Dyson's got to say.'

*   *   *

The mine foreman was walking across the hollow towards the office with Gerry Forrester as Hills and Johnson rode up. Seeing the woman, Hills looked at Johnson, pursed his lips and rolled his eyes skywards. Johnson jerked his head towards the long side of the office, where glass sparkled in the short grass beneath the shattered window, and Hills nodded. Then they were alongside the building under that broken window and dismounting and, as Hills tied his mount and looked at the trampled ground, Dyson was hanging back to greet them and Forrester's widow — looking remarkably sprightly, George thought — ran up the steps into the office.

'What do you two want?'

'Doing Yancey Flint a favour. Him and Owen are all tied up learning the intricacies of law enforcement, so we thought we'd take a look around.'

Dyson looked at Hills with what George Johnson considered to be a suspiciously guarded expression, then swiftly wiped it out with a cynical smile.

'Isn't it a mite late?'

'Might learn something.'

'Like what?'

'Never can tell.'

'Laconic as hell, aren't you?'

'To the point,' Hills said. 'Can we come in?'

Dyson grunted, and led the way up the steps. At the far end of the office, near the gaping iron safe, Gerry Forrester was sitting at a table. When she saw the two ex-lawmen, she put down her pencil and slid a blank sheet of paper over the one she'd been writing on. The table, George noticed, was riddled with holes. He and Hills removed their hats.

'My condolences, ma'am,' Frank Hills said. 'Murdering a man for money is a terrible thing to do.'

'Brutal,' Gerry Forrester said, 'but it wasn't exactly the perfect marriage,' and her blue eyes looked challengingly at Hills.

'Still and all,' Hills said, and shook his head. Dyson had gone to stand beside the woman. His hand rested on her shoulder, and George saw the strong fingers tighten, the woman's almost imperceptible nod.

'In Sid Tweddle's office,' Hills said, walking slowly down the long room with his eyes ranging, 'you didn't answer when I asked where you were when this happened.'

'I got here,' Dyson said tightly, 'but too late. By the time I kicked that door in the Geoghegans had stuffed the money in sacks, and Forrester was dead.'

'Is that why the safe's open, to convince us it's all gone?'

'No point shutting an empty safe, and you weren't expected,' Dyson said, frowning.

No, but you saw us coming, George thought, remembering how the woman had run quickly into the office.

'You say they clubbed Forrester to the floor,' Hills said, 'then shot him twice in the back of the head?'

'Right. I heard the shots. That's what brought me running. I let them have both barrels of a scatter-gun, but the bearded one, Sean, he was fast, used the table as a shield . . . ' He shrugged.

66

'Reckon you hit any of them?'

'Maybe. Be surprised if I missed entirely. But they were on their way out, so it was hard to tell.'

'Through that window?'

'I'd say that's obvious.'

'If they were already on their way out, how d'you know they knocked Forrester down before shooting him?'

Gerry Forrester's eyes narrowed. A faint flush coloured her cheeks. Dyson was grinning, but his dark eyes were cold and his rawboned frame was as tense as a coiled spring.

'The man had been gun whipped. He was bleeding, his cheekbone slashed open. Me, I'd say that happened first, then they shot him — but maybe you have other ideas?'

'Like what?' George Johnson said.

'Like, maybe the Geoghegans weren't here at all. Isn't that the first idea a naturally suspicious lawman would come up with?'

'For God's sake!' Gerry Forrester breathed.

'No,' Frank Hills said, 'that idea didn't occur to me. Someone was here, by the look of the ground where we dismounted, and George was with those Geoghegans long enough to know they planned a robbery. They were a bit too crafty for us, that's all.'

'And it'll get them nowhere.' Dyson eased his shoulders, visibly relaxing, let his hand fall from the woman's shoulder.

'Except very rich,' Gerry Forrester said, and the tip of her tongue moistened her lower lip.

Dyson shrugged and leaned against a table. 'It's only money,' he said, and George thought he detected a note of warning in the man's tone. 'Harold's bringing a replacement payroll in by stage, the men will get paid, the mine will keep pushing on into the hillside.'

'Sure, it's only money to you because it's not yours,' Hills said. 'But with the first safely stashed, that replacement payroll leaving Deadwood is going to look mighty attractive to the Geoghegans. Make 'em twice as rich, as compared to just very rich.'

Gerry chuckled. 'But they're not going to get their hands on it.'

'One robbery makes a second much harder.' Dyson shook his head, and it seemed to George he was trying too hard to explain the widow's words. 'There'll be a guard on the stage; Dewey Scaggs is the regular driver and tough as old leather, and Yancey Flint will have armed men watching the bank.'

'Nice to be so confident.' Hills let the words hang, gathering new meaning as each second passed, and George smiled inwardly, turned away and headed for the door. As he creaked down the steps he could hear the murmur of voices, and knew Distant was indulging in pleasantries, smoothing the waters, so to speak. Or maybe lulling Dyson and the woman into a false sense of security for, as sure as dogs barked at cats and lifted a leg to pee, there was something awful wrong in there.

His eyes looked along the side of the

building, and he pictured the Geoghegan Brothers coming out of the window
in a shower of glass, piling onto their
horses and heading . . . heading where?
A grassy slope led away from the
hollow, and George followed it with his
eyes to where the makings of a trail
emerged to fully form and snake
through the trees and up to the high
bluff he and Distant had skirted on
their way in.

'Up there,' Frank Hills said at his
shoulder. 'If we want answers, that's
where we go next.'

6

Dusk was an hour away. Fresh logs had been thrown on the camp-fire, and thick white smoke was being whipped up into the rattling willows and torn ragged by the freshening breeze. Somewhere in the foothills a coyote howled, the sound holding like a drawn-out sob of agony until carried away into a fragile, aching silence by the restless wind.

As the crackling fire was being banked, Padraig Geoghegan had expressed his deep concern: if there is a posse out there, he had complained, they sure as hell will see that smoke. But there was no fazing an ebullient Sean. Young Jimmy had taken hold of a raw plan that had shown promise but fallen short of brilliance, wrapped it up and neatly tied the loose ends. His uncomplicated mind had seen the obvious — take the stage, not the bank — and Sean was convinced that their earlier work on George Johnson would have left lawmen in Hannahan's Lode so confused that the obvious would almost certainly be overlooked.

'They won't dare leave town,' he said. 'My God, didn't we tell them we'd rob the bank, and didn't they watch it like hawks when we were out there robbing the mine? D'you seriously think after being fooled like that they'll protect the stage and leave the bank exposed?'

They'd slept in the shade for several hours after the good-natured fracas that had seen Jimmy Geoghegan ceremoniously dunked in the river, left Padraig with a purple welt under his eye and Sean nursing bruised ribs, eaten when they awoke, and were now restlessly going over their plans for the morrow. On such occasions — and there had been several during the past year — it was Padraig who was the worrier, the brother who picked holes in ideas put forward by Sean. Jimmy was the listener, the blue-eyed youngster who smiled a distant smile and often walked away into the deepening shadows while the others talked.

It was on one of those absences that Sean said, 'It'll be just the two of us taking the stage.'

'Are you serious? And after him coming up with the idea?'

'I have a bad feeling. It's the right thing to do, I know that, and surely less dangerous than riding into town to take the bank. But convincing myself those lawmen will overlook the obvious means I'm disregarding the vagaries of human nature. What if they hold talks, just like this? What if the consensus is that it's the bank they must guard, but one dissenter walks away — just as Young Jimmy has walked off — and takes with him like minded men who see things in a different light?'

'There's fifty miles between Deadwood and the Lode. The stage will set out soon after sun-up. We could hit it anywhere.'

'If this dissenter comes with his men, they'll start at the mine. With a Crow scout along with them it won't be too hard to pick up tracks at the bluff and find our old camp. Indeed, if George Johnson is with them they'll already know it. From there . . . '

He paused as Jimmy strolled in from the gathering dusk, the flickering fire lighting the soft planes of his young face.

'From there they'll have no trouble following our trail, wherever we go,' Jimmy said, moving closer and hunkering down by the fire, hands extended to the warmth. 'But isn't time something you're forgetting? Time dictates where the stage will be along that route, so we must choose our time carefully. And time is on our side; if they use their eyes to follow us, darkness will stop these men in their tracks, leaving them behind us by some eight hours.'

'In that case,' Sean said, 'choosing our time means the sooner the better.'

'As I understand these things,'

Padraig said, 'the driver of the stage and his guard will be the least apprehensive and the least watchful when they are still within a few miles of Deadwood. That's where it should be hit. But to do that — to hit it soon after sun-up — we must ride through the night.'

'So you see what I mean by time?' Jimmy said. 'It'll be dawn before anybody coming after us picks up the trail and follows it here, but already they'll be too late.'

Padraig, sitting back from the flickering circle of light that was being constricted by the encroaching shadows, had packed and lit his corncob pipe. As he nodded slowly at Jimmy's words and the smoke from the pipe curled around his face, he looked like a wise old medicine man with a straggly white beard. Sean grinned. Padraig, the worrier, appeared satisfied. If Paddy thought it was right, then it *was* right — and Sean could spot no flaws in the Young Jimmy's thinking, intelligent thinking that might one day usurp his

75

own position as leader. Well, good luck to the lad. Men quickly grew old. New blood was always needed. He shifted his gaze, saw Jimmy watching him, the firelight glinting in his blue eyes.

'I wasn't too far away to hear,' Jimmy said, and Sean grunted.

'And what I said about two of us making the raid makes sense?'

'Not at all.'

'It does,' Padraig said from the shadows. 'But then again, it does not.'

'Then I'll need reasons from both of you,' Sean said, 'and you, Young Jimmy, can have the privilege of speaking first.'

'The Geoghegan Brothers,' Jimmy said. 'There's three of them, everybody knows that. If two are there holding up the stage with masks over their faces, they'll know the third can't be too far away.'

'But even if they know that,' Sean said, 'my point is that the third man, the youngest of the bunch, will still be far enough away not to get himself killed.'

'Ah,' Jimmy said. 'I've a feeling that's not quite what you had in mind for me in the first place, but now you put it that way, it does make sense: I ride with you, but when we get close to the wagon trail out of Deadwood I drop back a conservative distance that serves a double purpose. Knowing there's a third man out there will make that shotgun guard cautious — but if he does make a move because he's unaware that there are three Geoghegan Brothers, then the first shot from my rifle as it whistles past his ear will give him the bad news.'

'There's truth in all of that,' Sean said. 'But now then, what about you, Paddy?'

'I was thinking along the same lines, both for the same reason and for another.'

'Lord help us,' Sean breathed.

'You see, supposing Jimmy is out there at this convenient distance, if things do go wrong and he's unable to help in any way at all, why then, he's a free agent and at liberty to have a go at the stage himself some way further down the trail.'

'And delighted to do so,' Jimmy said, grinning, 'if only to provide the cash to get you two out of jail.'

'Good points, the both of them,' Sean said. 'Or was it three I heard?'

'Whether two or three,' Padraig said, 'if I can understand the convoluted reasoning that's another new plan we've come up with.'

'I'd prefer to look on it as a reworking of Sean's fine original,' Jimmy said. 'Oh, and by the way, I think it would be prudent for me to carry the proceeds from the first robbery with me.'

'Beautifully put, and as all of that was worked out in a democratic process and presented with due respect for my authority,' Sean said, 'there's no need of anyone paying a second visit to the river.'

'Nor the time or energy for it,' Jimmy said, moving towards the saddles and gunny-sack stacked under the trees. 'If you two battered old men are hitting the stage from Deadwood at dawn, we'd best be on our way.'

★   ★   ★

All the way up the snaking trail from Forrester's yard it was clear that riders had recently passed that way in one hell of a rush. Once they reached the thinner trees at the top of the bluff, Frank Hills was in no doubt from the tracks and droppings that they were three in number, and could only be the Geoghegans.

He pulled his sweating horse into the shade, drew rein and began rolling a cigarette. George Johnson joined him, reached into his saddle-bag for his canteen, and took a long, tepid drink.

'Stopped here, same as us,' Hills said.

'We're steppin' in their footprints all the way,' George said. 'Down there outside the office. On the way up. Here. So where next?'

Hills grunted. He fired up his cigarette, watched the smoke caught and pulled away in a thin skein by the warm breeze; looked through it to the peaks away to the north and west.

Pondering before making up his mind, George thought as he corked and stowed his canteen. He'd been working alongside Frank Hills for a couple of years, moving to law enforcement in Hannahan's Lode after a frustrating ten years as an incompetent cow puncher that ended with a badly broken leg. That couple of years wearing a badge had given him a valuable insight into the marshal's thought processes, and he knew that Hills would take his time before coming up with a short answer, then elaborating on it.

Concerning the Geoghegans' plans, George was tempted to stick in his own two cents' worth, but was still smarting from his mishandling of the undercover operation. Hills had been aware that his deputy was champing at the bit, keen to show his mettle after a long time living in the marshal's long shadow, and when he got wind of the Geoghegans he'd given him his head. And, despite being made to look foolish and ending up out of a job, he still generously maintained that the mistakes that led to the payroll robbery were down to Sean Geoghegan's skilful duplicity, not George's unbelievable gullibility.

'Fifty miles or so,' Hills said now, ruminating aloud. 'Dewey Scaggs is a reliable jehu, but it's a tough trail for a horse, never mind a stage and team. Leaves Deadwood. Hits the rough country. Slows down to a walk more often than not. Passes through so many ravines and gulches and arroyos where a man can hide, it could be ambushed almost anywhere.'

'What we don't know is which one Sean Geoghegan will choose,' George said. 'About all we do know is where they camped for a whole week. And we know they were heading back that way after the bank robbery.'

'Which never happened,' Hills said.

'Right,' George said, abashed. 'So what you're saying, I guess, is I was wrong again and they'll be someplace else.'

'Still and all, it'll be easy enough to follow 'em.'

'But?'

'Well, when we get where they're going, there's no saying they'll still be there.'

'Could be following tracks for days, always gettin' where they're goin' too late to catch them.'

'And all we've got is hours, not days,' Hills said.

He sat contentedly sucking on his cigarette while George wiped the sweat from his brow and turned his gaze west to the lofty heights of Bear Mountain for inspiration. He knew he'd been foolish to believe *anything* Sean Geoghegan had told him, but that was in the past. What he had to do now was make up for that wasted week. Most times, a man could work out what was likely to happen by looking at what he knew about a situation. He'd told Distant that all they knew was where the Geoghegans had been camped — but they knew much more than that.

'Be kinda foolish of the Geoghegans,' he said, still gazing at the mountains, 'to hit the stage when it's pulling into the Lode.'

'Right,' Hills said. 'If Yancey Flint's intent on guarding the bank, when that stage is due he'll have armed men on roofs, in doorways, skulking up alleys. The Geoghegans probably think we're still in the job, but the same reasoning applies.'

'But knowing they're unlikely to hit the stage close to the Lode doesn't help us,' George said, watching Hills, 'because there's fifty miles of rough country to be watched, and no tellin' where the stage will be at any particular time.'

'Except the one,' Hills said.

George pondered for a moment, then chuckled. 'Directly after it leaves Deadwood?'

'Ideal spot. Long way from Hannah-an's Lode and all those armed men. Stage leaves at dawn. Driver and guard fresh out of bed, one getting the feel of the reins, the other figurin' out where to put his shotgun while he lights his first cigarette.'

'If Sean Geoghegan thinks the same as us — '

'He will.'

' — then we've got them.'

'You up to it?'

'After what they did to me?' George grinned. 'Just watch my smoke.'

7

They came down from the bluff and rode north for fifteen miles, then moved off the rough trail into a thick stand of pines where eerie shadows brought with them welcome relief from the scorching sun and a carpet of needles provided a soft surface for unrolled blankets.

By then it was late afternoon. Knowing the Geoghegans would do nothing until dawn, Frank Hills and George Johnson spent the rest of the daylight hours in dozing, lazy chatting, the consumption of a last meal of cold jerky washed down with more tepid water, and some final thoughts on the workings of the owlhoot mind.

Frank Hills was of the opinion that because the Geoghegans were only comparatively recent arrivals from Ireland — three or four years, or so he'd heard — they would have a different way of thinking to men more accustomed to the ways of the West.

'It's like trying to outguess a fox,' he said once, as approaching dusk brought a dankness to the shadows under the pines, 'only a fox of a kind we've never come across before.'

George was inclined to agree, because he'd been taken in by three men with dark hair and laughing blue eyes who had treated him like a brother outlaw while lying through their flashing white teeth.

But did that mean that Frank Hills himself was now being taken in? Not, like George, by the Geoghegans' honeyed words, but by his own misreading of those wily, Irish minds; his assumption that the Geoghegan Brothers would do one thing, when they were merrily — and quite logically for men reasonably fresh from the Emerald Isle — setting out to do something entirely different.

George voiced those concerns.

'Maybe,' Hills said. 'But right now

it's the best we can do. And if all we do manage is to meet the stage coming out of Deadwood, at least it'll have an escort all the way to Hannahan's Lode.'

★   ★   ★

The ride through the night was an exhilarating but tiring push across rugged terrain lit by cold moonlight, the crisp night air quickly banishing the last traces of sleep from their senses, the need for caution in their riding — both because of the treacherous ground and the dangers that lay an indeterminate distance ahead — swiftly bringing their minds to a high state of alertness. The one spell of relief they allowed themselves and their horses was the thirty minutes or so it took them to come down from the wooded hills, ride into the silent streets of Silver City and talk to the sleepy operator in the telegraph office. A waste of time. There no news of the Geoghegans, nor anything singing through the wires from Hannahan's Lode to suggest Yancey Flint was setting up any operation to ensnare the raiders.

They left the balding operator to his lonely vigil and rode through a deserted main street lit by smoking oil lamps. In that dim light the bright wink of a badge could be seen as a tall man appeared in the doorway of the jail, and for the rest of the way through the town George could feel those eyes boring into his back.

Maybe Hills sensed his discomfort.

'If I was still wearing a badge I'd call in, let him know what we're up to. As it is . . .'

The warm lights of Silver City fell away behind them and once again they felt the brooding presence of the tall peaks. They rode on through foothills blanketed with trees, moving across the flanks of the high ground a couple of hundred feet above the rutted wagon trail along which the stage would come rattling, pushing north with Hills constantly looking for sign that the Geoghegans had passed that way. But the cold, clear moonlight was fading. Far away to the east across the flat plains of the Dakotas there was a faint lightening in the sky, but full dawn was still a couple of hours away, Deadwood a good twenty miles to the north.

'They'll let it get ten miles out of town,' Hills said, his cigarette glowing in the darkness as he uncannily read George Johnson's thoughts. 'That means that some ten miles from here, three men are going to be holed up waiting for a stage — and finding them's going to be the devil's own job.'

'You talked about us riding escort if we miss them,' George said. 'Well, one sure way of making sure we don't is to meet the stage as it leaves Deadwood. Dewey Scaggs won't object if we ride with him.'

'I'd like to stop the hold-up, not meet it head on. Could be Sean Geoghegan'll figure the easiest way of getting that payroll is to use a rifle to kill the guard

— and maybe the driver — from a distance. A company of cavalry riding with the stage wouldn't stop that.'

'Not their style.'

'Up to now. But killing Brad Forrester suggests they've got the taste for blood.'

'If it was them.'

Hills chuckled, and his saddle creaked in the darkness as he turned to look at Johnson.

'You didn't swallow Dyson's story?'

'The Geoghegans were at the mine, no doubt of that. But the shooting of Forrester doesn't ring true — and Dyson and that woman appear to be a sight too close.'

'So the Geoghegans got the payroll, and Dyson — or maybe the woman — saw it as a good chance to get rid of an unwanted husband?'

'That's one possibility.'

'All right, so Ed Dyson murdered Brad Forrester for the woman. That still leaves us with three owlhoots who robbed the Forrester Mining Company and are sure as hell going to stop the stage from Deadwood and — '

'Quiet!'

Hills broke off, looked at Johnson. Bridles jingled as both men drew rein.

'What?'

Johnson's head was cocked. 'I thought I heard a horse whicker.'

And then it came again, the soft whicker of a horse — this time immediately silenced.

'Someone slapped a hand over its muzzle,' Hills opined. 'How far?'

'Half a mile, maybe. Downslope.'

'Close to the wagon trail. Picked their spot, now they're sitting nice and cosy, waiting for the stage but already counting the money.'

George Johnson slid from the saddle, peered off into the gloom then drew his Winchester from its boot. With great care he checked the loads.

'Always a pleasure,' Frank Hills said softly, 'to watch an expert at work.'

'Had a good teacher,' Johnson said.

'Then now you've checked that rifle,

put it away. In this light we're not likely to see anything until we trip over those damned Geoghegans, and when we do that you'll need your pistol.'

'And here's one for you,' George said. 'There's less likelihood of tripping over them — or of them hearing us — if we're on foot, so climb down off your horse and prepare to do some walking.' And with that he reached into his saddle-bag for ties, loose-hobbled his horse and led it off into the trees.

As Hills was following suit they again heard the soft, distant whickering of a horse. Hills's face was a pale blur in the faint light, but George caught the flash of his teeth as he grinned.

'Not expecting us,' the ex-marshal said quietly, 'or they'd be more careful. Figure if there was a posse it would have hunted them down by now, so those worries have been put aside. All they're thinking of is that stage, and the fat payroll.'

'But if we come in from two sides, move about and do some yelling while letting loose with a few shots — '

'Yeah,' Hills said. 'The realization that you've been wrong and a posse's bearing down on you can be mighty intimidating. In those circumstances, I've seen panic turn a man's legs to water.'

Although the distant horse now remained silent, its earlier whickering had given both men a good idea of its location: downhill; some way to the north. Over favourable terrain that would have made the walking easy but, with sounds travelling far through the still air, a snapping twig would have given them away, they were forced to test the ground with each step, carefully brush aside trailing branches to avoid the brittle crack that would betray them, and all the time they were conscious of time slipping away and the stage that would soon be leaving Deadwood.

With the land falling away in wide, tree-carpeted ridges to their right and dawn still a pale promise lightening the skies to the east, eyesight was of little use. But the loss of one sense caused others to be heightened and, knowing this from experience, when he wasn't watching his footing George Johnson was sniffing the air and straining so hard to hear his ears ached. He could smell horses, but knew that scent lingered on his own hands and clothing; caught the musk odour of night animals, but discounted it; detected the heavy, masculine odour of fresh sweat from close by and for an instant was alarmed until he realized his shirt was so damp it was sticking to his back and allowed himself a soft, rueful chuckle.

Then he caught the faintest whiff of smoke, and reached out to touch Frank Hills's sleeve.

'Around the camp-fire, Padraig Geoghegan would always be smoking a corn cob,' he whispered, and jerked his thumb vaguely ahead and raised his face in an exaggerated sniff as Hills turned to him, his eyes glinting.

'Easy now,' Hills said, nodding understanding.

The skies were lighter. They had emerged silently from the trees and were on a ridge covered with coarse grass overlooking a steep slope leading to a rocky outcrop some fifty feet below and to their left. Beyond that outcrop's sheer drop the ground sloped easily to the twisting trail which, at that point, was conveniently fringed by thick stands of trees.

From that distance, looking around the outcrop, George could just make out the dark shapes of two horses; even as he did so, one of them blew softly, and an unseen man murmured gruffly.

'*Two* horses?' Hills said close to his ear.

'Back at the mine, Dyson used a scatter-gun. Maybe he put one of those Irish scoundrels out of action.'

Hills nodded. 'Works for us, if he did. And so does this set-up. They're down there with the horses, tight up against the rock, watching the trail. Reckon we can push on a hundred yards, then come down the slope onto that outcrop without being seen?'

'If we can,' George said, 'we'll come on them so fast and sudden we won't need to play posse.'

Hills took a breath, expelled it silently. 'Let's go.'

George drew his six-gun and went after Hills until they were above the outcrop, then followed him as he turned down the fifty-foot slope. It was grass all the way, a coarse carpet that deadened sound. Loose stones threatened to turn a man's ankle, but were easily avoided. Halfway down, the slope steepened, the descent became perilous. Out there in the open, the light was improving by the minute, and that and the altered angle afforded them a view over the edge. Hills lifted a hand in warning. George froze, followed Hills's gaze and saw the crown of a Stetson, a thin cloud of pipe smoke; another dark-bearded man, standing. But that second man had his back to them as he gazed towards the Deadwood trail. Cautiously, Hills resumed his descent. George eased his sweating hand on the butt of six-gun, and followed.

And, on the dew-soaked grass, his feet shot from under him.

He hit the ground on his back, jarred his right elbow and, as pain knifed to his shoulder, his six-gun blasted. The muzzle flash was dazzling, the sound of the shot a brittle crack that fluttered through the trees and echoed thinly across the high slopes. Sliding on his back on the slick grass, legs and arms out, heels and clawed fingers fighting for grip, George slammed into a startled Frank Hills and knocked him flat. Then, as Hills rolled, grabbed for his arm and missed, George was at the outcrop's edge. Wet grass became hard rock that tore the skin from his elbows. The sharp rock edge was an unyielding ridge grinding the small of his back as legs and hips slid over and dragged him into emptiness. Suddenly he was weightless. Cold air slapped at his sweating face. A thin squeak was dragged from his lungs, became a drawn out wail that was abruptly chopped off as he landed astride one of the Geoghegans saddled horses with a jolt that threatened to crush his manhood and sent a wave of sickening pain flooding into his belly.

Time seemed to stand still, yet around him in what could have been no more than a single frozen moment there was pandemonium. A second horse was squealing, backing and rearing against a tight tether, eyes white and wild. Sean Geoghegan had spun, dropped into a crouch and gone for his six-gun, and on his bearded face there was a startled look that was almost comical as he saw George struggling to stay aboard the panicked, rearing horse. Padraig Geoghegan was coming to his feet, but it was like watching a man in slow motion. He came away from the rock face where he had been sitting, half turned towards George, reached up to take the corncob pipe from his mouth while his other hand moved lazily to the pistol at his hip, and all this seemed to take an age as time hung suspended and the Geoghegans — after those first instinctive movements — stood frozen in shock.

Atop the pitching horse George realized that despite bloody elbows and the agony in his belly he was still in one piece, his Stetson was still tight on his head, his fingers were still clutching his six-gun in a grip of iron.

'Stand still!' he yelled, cocking the pistol as his voice cracked. 'Drop those guns and back off.' And, as the ache in his guts forced bile up into his throat, he kicked the horse violently in the ribs, sawed on the reins and held the quivering animal still.

'Would you believe it,' Sean Geoghegan said, 'it's our friend and fellow outlaw, George Johnson.'

'Seeing as he's been good enough to drop in on us,' Padraig said, 'why don't we invite him to step down?'

'Ah, but a man once bitten is twice

shy,' Sean said. 'Him arriving like this is highly suspicious, so maybe it'd be better to plug him where he sits.'

'But not before we talk to him, ask him what he's doing here when all good men are still in their beds.'

'But George is not just a good man, he's Frank Hills's deputy,' Sean said. 'Tell me, George, why are you not wearing your badge?'

And so the shock was over. Sean Geoghegan relaxed and cast a quick glance over his shoulder to assure himself that the stage was not in sight. Padraig had restored the corn cob to his mouth, and was standing with his six-gun at his side as he closely watched George.

But they were as loquacious as ever, George realized, talking because that was what came naturally to them, talking because, maybe, it helped them to think, but at the same time acting as if the six-gun in his hand was a child's harmless toy carved from a hunk of wood. They had fooled him once over the bank raid and, despite the suspicions Sean had voiced, they were unable to take him seriously. The way around that, George decided, was to show them the error of their ways.

Casually, without seeming to take aim, he pulled the trigger and blew the six-gun from Padraig Geoghegan's hand. Sean Geoghegan recoiled as the slug ricocheted and whined past his ear. Padraig roared, and shook his numbed fingers. The pistol hit the hard ground and bounded down the slope.

Then both men recovered. Sean took a step sideways and snapped a shot that cracked into the rock face alongside George and again set the terrified horse pitching and sent George's answering shot winging harmlessly skywards. Padraig ducked back against the rock, came up from the heaped saddle-bags and gunny-sack with a Winchester and jacked a shell into the breech and fired all in one swift, smooth movement. George's Stetson flew into the air. He felt his scalp rip, and hot blood trickled onto his ear. And as he fought to stay in the saddle and bring his six-gun to bear on one of the dancing, shifting Geoghegans, he saw Sean's face split in a grin of pure delight as he lifted his six-gun, levelled it at George and his finger went bone-white on the trigger.

'Hold it right there!' Frank Hills roared, and stones rattled down the rock face as he appeared on the edge of the outcrop with a gleaming pistol in his fist. 'Throw down those guns or, so help me, I'll drop both of you where you stand.'

8

Dewey Scaggs eased his grip on the three pairs of reins, shifted the plug of tobacco from one whiskery cheek to the other, spat a stream of brown liquid and squinted sideways at the guard.

'Beats me,' he said, 'why they keep this damn coach a-runnin'. Railroad's taken over, most trips we ain't got one damn traveller, and if they're about to use it for transportin' cash money then I reckon they can find them another damn driver.'

'You finished bellyachin'?'

Mick East was a bone-thin drifter who'd offered his services as shotgun guard because the pay for the single trip from Deadwood to the Lode meant he got where he wanted to go, and ended up with cash in his pocket. His horse was trotting behind the ancient Concord. His bedroll was in the box. The fact that a sack containing the payroll for the Forrester Mining Company was in the rear boot worried him not one jot.

'Hah!' Scaggs said, and settled his battered hat firmly on his ragged mop of white hair as the stage hit a stony downslope and picked up speed. 'You any idea why we're carryin' that payroll?'

'It's goin' from here to there,' East said, grinning, 'and it sure as hell can't walk.'

'You heard of them damn Geoghegans?'

'Sure. Doin' what the James boys did twenty years ago, only with more style.'

'Style, be damned. Only yesterday they murdered Brad Forrester, made off with the cash money intended for the fellers workin' his mine. What we're carryin' ain't just a payroll, it's a *replacement* payroll — and you think them damn Geoghegan Brothers won't know it?'

East frowned. 'There'll be a posse

out hunting them. That'll keep them well away, drive them deep into the hills.'

'Not so. The way I hear, a dandified new marshal by the name of Yancey Flint figures they'll hit John Kennedy's bank in the Lode. He's so damn lazy he's settin' tight, waitin' for them to come to him so's he can blow their damn heads off.'

'And you ain't so sure they will?'

Again Scaggs spat a stream of juice. 'What would you do if you was in the business of robbery? On the one side you kin see a bank tucked away in the middle of town, staked out by a dozen armed men. On the other you kin see a stage, an old-timer holdin' the reins, jest one nervous feller settin' beside him with a shotgun.'

'I ain't nervous,' East said.

'No,' Dewey Scaggs said, 'but if I was in your boots I damn well would be.'

They rode in silence for the next couple of miles, rocking with the swaying coach, East with his hand on the shotgun and his eyes looking ahead as the skies brightened and the first dazzling rays of the rising sun reached the thick woodland lining the rutted track and stretching away to blanket the foothills.

Just his damned luck. He'd picked the one coach out of Deadwood with no passengers, carrying a fat payroll to dangle like a juicy carrot in front of the Geoghegan Brothers. Three Irish renegades, in the area, and already fired up with one more successful robbery under their belts.

Well, maybe that was enough for them. Scaggs had Yancey Flint figuring they'd go for the coach and not the bank, but both men could be a mile out in their thinking. With cash from the mine safe in their saddle-bags, why would the Irish bandits risk going up against a shotgun? Move on, that's what East would do. Catch some other lazy bastards by surprise, in some other sleepy town.

He fished the makings out of his vest

pocket, offered the sack to Scaggs who just turned his head and spat another stream of brown juice. East shrugged, dropped his hand to feel the shiny barrel of the shotgun resting up against his thigh, then leaned back and began rolling a cigarette.

And the bullet that came screaming down the trail took paper and sack clean out of his hands, plucked at the shirt under his arm on the way through and slammed into the body of the swaying Concord.

'Jesus!' East said, spitting shreds of tobacco and poking a finger at the hole in his shirt.

'It's them damn Geoghegans,' Scaggs shouted, and his big gnarled hands tightened on the reins.

'Keep going!'

'Hah!'

Even as Scaggs mouthed his derision and slammed a foot on the brake lever, East saw there was no way out, no way through. The single masked figure was seated on his horse, sideways on in the middle of the track some forty yards ahead. A Winchester rifle was at his shoulder, a trickle of smoke issuing from the muzzle. The stage could run him down, drive on through, no problem there. But East knew that if it did, it would go rattling on down the trail to Hannahan's Lode with no driver, and no guard.

On the rims of the big back wheels the brake blocks were smoking. The six-horse team was fighting the traces, feeling the weight of the coach pushing them while the ornery jehu was heaving on the ribbons and ordering them to halt. In the end they did so, jostling in the traces with tossing heads as the coach groaned to a stop behind them and, in a stink of brake blocks and hot oil, a cloud of dust drifted ahead to swirl like cannon smoke around the unmoving bandit.

'Thought there were three of them?' East muttered.

'One to stop us,' said Dewey Scaggs, raising his voice and glaring at the armed horseman, 'two hid somewhere in them damn trees.'

'So keep that thought in your mind and the shotgun right where it is,' the masked bandit said, walking his horse forward. 'There's one of my brothers on either side, you've got nowhere to go, nowhere to turn — so you, driver, step down, walk around the back and lift that nice heavy sack out of the boot for me.'

'Ain't no sack,' Scaggs said.

Still keeping the Winchester level and steady, the horseman reached up to adjust the bandanna across the bridge of his nose. A glint of anger showed in his dark eyes. He stared at Scaggs, waited, let the silence press heavily on the old jehu.

'Went last night,' Scaggs said, flicking a glance at Mick East. 'Special wagon, with escort. You're too damn late, Irish.'

'And as it's all night I've been sitting here,' the bandit said, 'I know full well you're telling me lies. Open the boot, old man, save yourself a lot of pain.'

Nobody moved. East tried to swallow, found no spit in his dry mouth, listened to his pulse hammering in his ears and narrowed his eyes to squint off into the distance. One of the horses snorted, moved restlessly. Alongside East, Scaggs chuckled softly and settled back on the box. The reins were looped easily over his big knuckles. His foot still pushed down hard on the brake lever.

When East let his gaze drop nervously to the bandit, he saw the sheen of sweat on the man's forehead.

Eyes ugly, the bandit kneed his horse forward. He came around the nervous team and alongside East. With the Winchester muzzle boring into the guard's belly, he reached across for the shotgun and hurled it to the ground. He looked over at Scaggs, saw that no gunbelt encircled the old man's lean hips, and backed off to ease his horse alongside of the Concord.

Scaggs looked at East. East looked nervously into Scaggs's sharp blue eyes, and saw what was in the man's mind. He opened his mouth, figured he had something to say but couldn't get the words out. He managed a dry swallow, watched the old jehu's big hands lift the reins delicately, felt his eyes drawn to the man's braced right leg and the stovepipe boot holding the brake lever.

Then, at the back of the coach, the bandit's Winchester blasted. The horses leaped and milled in the traces, ears flattened. As the Concord jerked, East nearly fell off the box. Metal tinkled as the shattered lock hit the ground. And as hinges squealed and the unseen bandit raised the boot's lid, Dewey Scaggs jerked his foot back off the brake lever and flicked the reins.

The team leaped forward. The traces snapped tight. The Concord rocked backwards on the oxhide thorough-braces, then heaved forwards and the whole rig was in motion, rocking and rattling down the track as Mick East curled up on the box and closed his eyes and Dewey Scaggs stood with braced legs and screamed his encouragement to horses that had their heads high and were running like the wind.

The noise abated. The thunder of hooves and the creaking of wood and leather faded into the distance. The coach was lost against the distant trees in a drifting cloud of dust. The bandit slid the knotted bandanna off his face and down around his neck, spat, grinned happily, then heaved the heavy gunny-sack up across his thighs and rode off the trail and into the thick trees.

9

'Where's Jimmy?'

In the lee of the rock face the dazzling light of the rising sun slanted across the tops of the tall trees to touch Sean Geoghegan's face and create brilliant highlights in his dancing blue eyes. He shook his head at Johnson's question, put on a grave face and stroked his black beard.

'Now, George, did you not see the blood in Forrester's office? We've not denied we were there, and when he burst in on us that bastard Dyson let loose with his shotgun. You know Jimmy would be here with us, if he could. As it is, he's been forced to remain back in our camp by the river . . .'

Sean broke off, let the missing words tell their own tragic message as he looked sombrely at his grim-faced brother.

'We saw the blood all right,' Frank Hills said. 'A pool of it, alongside Brad Forrester's head.'

'He'll be right as rain. The man's got a thick skull, a tap on the cheek will do him no lasting harm.'

'The two bullets you put in the back of the head have done permanent damage — '

'No!' Padraig Geoghegan shook his head. 'Not us. The man was alive when we rode away from the mine, there's not a one of us would do such a terrible thing.'

'But it was done.'

Sean looked at Hills, his narrowed eyes suddenly speculative. 'Who, then? Someone close to home maybe, taking advantage of a situation? I've mentioned no name, but I could surely point you to one conniving bastard who might steal the fat payroll for himself — a payroll we never even got a sniff of.'

George caught Frank Hills swift look, and knew the ex-marshal was remembering their conversation. On the ride

114

across country from the mine, Hills had listened intently while George voiced suspicions over Dyson's involvement in the Forrester shooting, and a while later suggested that one of the renegade brothers might have been laid low by Dyson's scatter-gun. Surely it was stretching coincidence for the Geoghegans to come up with the identical reason for Jimmy's absence if it wasn't true, and follow that with identical suspicions about Dyson?

But what had happened to the payroll? Ed Dyson? Perhaps. The Geoghegans? Well, the suggestion that they'd not got a sniff of it was stretching credulity — but everything these bandits had told George in the days and nights he had spent with them had carried with it the ring of truth, and look where that had left him!

The same thought seemed to have occurred to Frank Hills.

Abruptly, he said, 'Search their saddle-bags.'

The horses were saddled; going

through the bags took less than a minute. George turned away as he fastened the last buckle, looked across at Hills and shook his head.

'Then Jimmy Geoghegan has it.'

'It would be an awful long ride,' Sean Geoghegan said, 'to discover your mistake.'

'Has to be done,' Hills said. 'Three Geoghegan Brothers robbed the Forrester Mining Company. Could be those same three brothers had a hand in Brad Forrester's murder. So tonight, it'll be three brothers — not two — I'll be locking up in one of those strap-steel cells in Hannahan's Lode.'

'Ah, but it's come to my notice,' Sean Geoghegan said, 'that neither you nor our fine friend George is wearing a badge. If you have no badge you have no jail, and no cells.'

'Yancey Flint and Buck Owen are marshal and deputy now. We'll get you to town, they'll take over.'

'But isn't it true that you need some authority to move us at all?'

'Authority?' Hills's laugh was a short, no nonsense bark. 'Here's my authority,' he said, slapping a hand against his filled holster, 'and there's your last hope of salvation,' and he pointed to the gunbelts and rifles that George had removed and dumped against the cliff when Hills had appeared so suddenly on the edge of the outcrop. 'Now, no more talk. It's half a mile to our horses, most of it uphill. We ride, you walk. And if you make a break for it — well, I'd just as soon take you in belly-down as upright in the saddle and on the prod.'

★   ★   ★

'Here she comes!'

Buck Owen was at the door of the jail, Stetson tugged down as he squinted into the sun and almost danced in his excitement as white-haired Dewey Scaggs stood at the reins and swung the stage from Deadwood into Hannahan's Lode and brought it rattling down the length of the street to the square.

Yancey Flint sighed. He'd just fired up a fat cigar, settled his boots on the desk and reached for a fat wad of Wanted dodgers so that he would look busy if Sid Tweddle walked across the street and poked his head in the door. When he finally dragged himself upright, carefully balanced the smouldering cigar on the edge of an ashtray, settled his white Stetson on his head, adjusted the hand of his ivory-handled six-guns, polished the badge on his vest with his sleeve and smoothed the droop of his thick moustache outwards with wetted finger and thumb as he walked tall and elegant to join his deputy, he saw that his caution had been justified: Councillor Sidney Tweddle was angling across the square, as awkward on his feet as a fat black crow, coughing and spluttering as he waddled through the cloud of dust dragged along in the wake of the coach that was now juddering to a halt outside John Kennedy's bank.

'Flint, Owen!' Tweddle yelled, 'get yourselves over here, watch over this payroll going into the bank.'

Owen broke into a jog, drawing his six-gun. Yancey Flint wandered towards the old Concord stage in a style more befitting a town marshal, and got there in time for sprightly Dewey Scaggs to leap down from the box, throw a scornful look at the tall man with the badge pinned to his vest and send a stream of tobacco juice dangerously close to the new marshal's polished boots.

'Where's Frank Hills?'

'Forget Hills. I'm town marshal, Buck's my deputy — '

'God help us all!'

'Never mind that,' Tweddle said, lumbering up with a big white handkerchief fluttering as he mopped his glistening brow. 'Act lively now, get that cash into the bank before the Geoghegan Brothers ride into town and snatch it from under our noses.'

'Take it easy,' Flint said. 'They'll

come when the money's safe inside and they figure everyone's asleep, most likely at dawn tomorrow — '

'You know that for certain?'

'That's what they told George Johnson, only to fool him they juggled the dates. This time you've got the right man in the job.'

'If you'd been doing the job I hired you for, the Geoghegans would be behind bars.'

'They'll come soon enough. We'll be ready, and I'll put them away,' Flint said.

The bone-thin drifter jumped down from the box, shotgun in one lean hand, and squinted sideways at Scaggs with a cynical grin.

'Just like you said.'

'Sure. The new marshal's settin' with his feet up, waitin' to shoot them damn bandits' heads off.'

'Only he's too late.'

'Too late!' Sid Tweddle's eyes were bulging. Behind him, a tall, dark-suited figure had emerged from the bank.

Tweddle turned that way, took a couple of faltering steps, flapped his hands in a plump shooing motion. 'John, you step back inside to your business, I'll handle this, look after the cash.' He waited, saw the tall banker nod and step back inside, then swung on Scaggs and said in a furious undertone, 'What the hell do you mean, too late?'

'We were robbed, ten, fifteen miles out of Deadwood.'

'Robbed?' Tweddle spluttered. 'But . . . but . . . '

'Ain't no buts,' Scaggs said. 'Payroll's gone. Them damn Geoghegans took it.'

'You mean . . . ' Sid Tweddle's sweating face was purple. His glare switched to the speechless Yancey Flint, the gaping Buck Owen. 'You mean, Mr Scaggs, that while my town marshal and his deputy were sitting on their backsides, the Geoghegan Brothers coolly held up the stage outside Deadwood and took the Forrester Mining Company's payroll?'

Scaggs looked at the guard as if for

reassurance, his face comically perplexed. 'Ain't that what I just said?'

'Sure was. We were robbed, that's what you said.'

'For God's sake!' Tweddle fumed. 'I'm not deaf, I know what you said. What I want to know is how a bunch of Irish bandits can rob the Deadwood stage when — ' He broke off, clenched his teeth, and turned on Yancey Flint. 'This is your fault, Marshal.'

Flint narrowed his eyes, puffed his chest and manfully squared his shoulders. 'No, sir, it's the fault of Hills and Johnson, those bandits have had them tied in knots right from the start of this mess. Luckily, you've two good men on the job — '

'No,' Tweddle said, shaking his head as he stiffly walked a few paces away to gather his composure, swivelled angrily and walked back. 'I'm afraid I addressed you incorrectly, Flint. You have a shiny tin badge, but you are not this town's marshal, not until the council approves my recommendation.

Well, let me tell you, unless the payroll is recovered and the Geoghegans brought to justice — '

'Riders coming,' Buck Owen called.

Dewey Scaggs who, with the lean drifter, had climbed back onto the box and was preparing to move the stage and its weary team down to the livery barn, now stood up and peered back down the street over the top of the Concord.

'It's that there Hills and Johnson you were talkin' about,' he said, 'and it looks like they've got theirselves a couple of damn prisoners.'

'By God!' Tweddle breathed, 'so they have.'

The four riders came at an easy trot down the opposite side of the street, entered the square with bridles jingling and dust spurting from hooves as they headed for the jail. Hills looked across at the stage and the men clustered around it, said something to George Johnson, then turned to the dark-bearded man whose feet were lashed together under the belly of his horse.

'Sean Geoghegan,' Tweddle said, and started ploughing across the square. 'By hell, he's got him!'

Yancey Flint jerked his head at Buck Owen, and opened his long legs to follow the sweating, puffing councillor. Owen moved alongside, almost jogging to keep up.

'Makes us look kinda sick, Yancey.'

'Does it? Keep your fingers crossed, pal. Last I heard, there were three Geoghegans. I don't see but two.'

'Yeah, but if Hills has got the payroll — '

'If.'

By the time they'd crossed the square, Hills and Johnson had arrived outside the jail, were out of the saddle, and with the horses at the rail and hitched were untying the outlaws' bindings. Tweddle had staggered the final few yards to reach them, but was now leaning forward with his hands braced on his thighs, too breathless to speak.

'Sid looks plumb tuckered out,' Hills said, as Yancey Flint approached. 'He been running behind you with a sharp stick to prod you awake?'

'Probably exhausted himself lifting Yancey Flint out of your chair,' George Johnson said, straight faced, 'when he caught sight of you riding into town with them two Geoghegans.'

'Just *two* Geoghegans?' Flint said, sneering. 'What happened, the other one too slippery for you?'

'Wounded and on the run, he won't get far,' Hills said.

'Indeed he won't,' Sid Tweddle said, straightening with difficulty and mopping his face. 'But the main thing is you caught two of the scoundrels and recovered the payroll — '

'Payroll?' Hills jerked around as Sean Geoghegan slid stiffly from the saddle.

'Ah, Paddy,' the bearded bandit said, beaming, 'we agreed it was a fine plan from the beginning, but hasn't the youngster reworked it to perfection?'

'Reworked it with a touch of genius,

and carried it out like a true Geoghegan,' said Padraig.

'Jesus Christ!' Hills said. 'The stage has been robbed?'

'And you haven't got the money,' Sid Tweddle said, his voice had the hollow resonance of an empty coffin.

Yancey Flint chuckled, and shook his head. 'My, my, Sid, didn't I tell you the Geoghegans had Hills and Johnson tied in knots? Like fools they watched the bank when the mine was being robbed then, through sheer good luck, they catch two of the Geoghegans but let the third get away with another payroll.'

Tweddle glared. 'And you could do better?'

'Could, but can't,' Flint said airily. 'Without town council approval of my position as marshal and Buck as my deputy, my hands are tied.'

10

'I've spoken to the miners,' Ed Dyson said, 'told them the stage from Deadwood should be getting close to the Lode with the replacement payroll. I've told them the company's New York backer is behind them all the way. They're at work in the diggings, still complaining, still threatening to walk away from the job. But they'll see today out, because I've told them pay day's arranged for tomorrow morning.'

'Stupid fools!'

Gerry Forrester was not looking at Dyson, so was unable to see the strangely detached look in his dark eyes. She was bending over the polished table, the light from the window glinting on her flaxen hair. In front of her were three gunny-sacks. The one he had carried in — after tethering his lathered horse but leaving the rig in place — was open, and she was running her fingers through the pile of bills that had spilled onto the table.

'No. They're hard, practical men, and dangerous if they get wind of what's going on.'

'And what is going on?' She looked up at the tall man standing by the stone fireplace with the dust of the trail on his dark clothing, speculation in her blue eyes. 'Yesterday you acted fast when the Geoghegans came down from the hills and burst in on Brad. Today you out-thought them, beat them at their own game. I'm proud of you, what you've done: as far as anyone knows, the Geoghegans are on the loose with three sacks of money — and we've got maybe eighteen hours.'

'Eighteen?'

'That's right. Eighteen hours to make up our minds before those miners realize there is no money. Eighteen hours start on anyone who might come after us — but only if we decide now. Or your last eighteen hours of freedom if you slip up and word of this gets out.' The speculation in her eyes had been replaced by a hint of amusement. 'If that happens they'd put you away for a long time, Ed.'

Dyson had been rolling a cigarette. He lit it, thoughtfully trickled smoke from his nostrils, nodded slowly and followed it with his expressionless dark eyes as it rose and flattened into a thin cloud against the low ceiling.

'We never did take it any further than wishful thinking, did we?' he said. 'You hated Brad, because the man you married became a stranger as soon as the organ music faded. I had nothing against him, but every month I watched those money sacks thump onto his desk and dreamed about what might be.' He wet the tip of his finger, touched it to the glowing end of the cigarette, pursed his lips and lifted his eyes to the woman. 'And now you're asking me what's going on.'

'Yes.'

'And telling me if I slip up they'll put

me away for a long time — because, of course, you're the grieving widow. They'd ask questions, but you'd come up with the right answers and, anyway, nobody would believe you had anything to do with murder and robbery.'

She shrugged.

'Which makes me wonder why, if all the risks are mine, any of this money should be yours.'

She had been stuffing the bills back into the sack. Now her head snapped up, her eyes flashing.

'We're in this together. You agreed.'

'When? I just told you, we never did go beyond wild dreams.'

'That was enough. They excited us. We understand each other, we want the same things.'

'The same *thing*. Money. And there it is.' He jerked his head at the table.

Her hands tightened on the sack. 'If we leave now,' she said, 'we can be riding a Pullman by nightfall, on our way to New York.'

He shook his head. 'When they

realize what we've done, that's the first place they'll look. They'll wire ahead. The railroad's a trap for a man on the run — '

'A man and a woman!'

'Better by far,' he said, head shaking, 'to ride the high country — '

'All right, we'll do that. I can ride as well as the next man, keep you warm when the nights are cold — '

'A man riding alone travels safer, faster.'

'Goddamn it!' she said softly, 'you think carefully about what you're doing, this money belongs to *my* family — '

'The Forrester family,' he said easily, and flicked the cigarette behind him into the empty grate, flexed his fingers. 'You married into it, that's all. Harold Forrester always held that against you. Now Brad's dead, you're out in the cold.'

She was watching his hand; the six-gun lashed to his thigh. The tip of her tongue came out, moistened her full lower lip. 'Ed, don't do this,' she said — and she stepped back from the table, looked wildly across the room to where gleaming rifles stood in a wall rack.

'It's easier than I thought it would be,' he said, and he was smiling as he drew his six-gun. 'Stepping over that invisible line's set me free.'

'No! Someone will hear. You'll never get away.'

'I told you,' he said, easing back the hammer. 'They're all up at the mine.'

'Don't!' she cried. 'Please. I won't say anything — '

'They'll put me away for a long time,' he echoed, 'if this gets out,' and his jaw clamped as he shook his head.

With a sudden lunge, she went around the table. Her arm swept across it, sweeping the sacks of money off the shiny surface. They fell heavily to the floor, skidded towards Dyson's planted feet, loose bills fluttering like moths in the shafts of sunlight. Gerry's flaxen hair flew loosely as she ran desperately towards the racked rifles — and the sharp crack of the pistol dragged a wailing cry from her open mouth that was instantly cut off as the bullet tore into her back, drove her forward, slammed her against the wall. One hand trailed across a shiny Winchester, dragging it with her as she slid to the floor. She twisted as she fell, rolled onto her back. Her blue eyes stared glassily, sightlessly, as he came and stood over her.

Ed Dyson sighed. He pouched the smoking six-gun, bent down and took hold of the dead woman's ankles and began to drag her towards the door. Her body left a streak of dark, wet blood on the boards. He pulled the door open, took a deep breath, then walked backwards across the gallery. When he took her down the steps the regular, loose thump of her head hitting the boards drew his teeth back in a wordless snarl.

And all the way around the house to the patch of tangled scrub where he dumped the body of the woman who had been a part of his dream, that snarl stayed fixed and ugly, the dark eyes as bleak as the future that held nothing for Ed Dyson but a heap of soiled, stolen money.

11

With the bad news delivered, Dewey Scaggs and his guard took the Concord rattling down one side of the square to the livery barn; on the other side, Buck Owen made a great show of pushing the two grinning Geoghegan Brothers into the jail and through to the cells while, in the front office, Yancey Flint sat down at the desk in a cloud of cigar smoke and proceeded to deal with the paperwork.

Not yet sure what was in Sid Tweddle's mind when he emerged, red-faced, from John Kennedy's bank, Frank Hills crossed the square with George Johnson to Jed Cooper's general store, passed ten minutes bringing the burly storekeeper up to date then went next door to the sagging café, and wolfed down a huge late breakfast cooked and served by Jed's wife.

Then, belts loosened, it was another walk back across the square to the welcome shade of Clancy's saloon. The beer was warm but wet, the big room cool after the dusty heat of the square, the natural light at the table dim enough to allow a trail-weary man to look about him without squinting. Perversely, Frank Hills kept switching his gaze to the window overlooking the dazzling brilliance of the square, and George Johnson knew he was still cogitating on what crumpled, sweating Sid Tweddle might be cooking up in the room over the newspaper office.

'What *can* he do?' George said, breaking into the silence. 'He can't pin badges on every citizen who brings in a couple of outlaws, no more than he can snatch them back off lawmen who are doing their job.'

'The lawmen doing the job,' Hills said, 'are the ones without the badge. Buck's jangling a bunch of keys, Yancey Flint's doing some scratching with a pen. And that's it. About all those two have done since yesterday is strut the square showing off their shiny tinware.' He took another drink, scowled, and said, '*Our* shiny tinware.'

'It'll be ours again,' George said, 'if we recover those payrolls.'

'But first we've got to find . . . ?' Hills shrugged, squinted sideways at George. 'You come up with any bright ideas on who robbed that stage? You reckon Jimmy Geoghegan, or what?'

'One man who might give us some pointers,' George said, 'has just walked in.'

As the swing doors slapped, Hills looked that way and called, 'Over here, Dewey.'

The old jehu limped across the sawdust, veered towards the bar to spit a stream of tobacco juice into a cuspidor, then came over to the two exlawmen and straddled a chair.

'Who's buyin'?'

'I'll get you one,' George said.

He left the two men talking. Coggins took time locating a glass and pouring, and George turned his back to the bar and rested his elbows. Whitehaired Dewey Scaggs had never been known as a taciturn man, and already he was talking volubly to Hills. But what did he have to say that would be of any value? The mouthful he'd spat out to the spluttering Sid Tweddle — 'Them damn Geoghegans took it' — was information, but it seemed to be false: at the time Scaggs and his guard were looking into the barrel of a gun, Sean and Padraig had been riding across country in a futile chase after Jimmy Geoghegan with George, and Frank Hills.

And, George thought ruefully, that other Geoghegan was still out there. As he took the tepid glass of beer from Coggins and carried it across to Scaggs, he was recalling the triumphant grins splitting the faces of the two prisoners when they heard the stage had been robbed. With Jimmy on the loose, that surely meant just one thing.

'The way Dewey saw the hold-up,'

Frank Hills said as George sat down, 'it was a classic. Two men either side of the trail ready to give covering fire for the third masked man with a rifle.'

'Not the way I *saw* it,' Scaggs growled, 'the way it happened. Feller shot a hole clear through Mick East's shirt, told us his brothers had us in their damn sights.'

'Geoghegans?'

'That's what he said.'

'You sure?'

Scaggs was scowling at George, his mouth open ready to chew his head off, when the swing doors slapped again and Sid Tweddle walked in followed by the lean man who'd ridden shotgun on the stage from Deadwood. Tweddle glared, and made for the bar. The guard saw Scaggs, and came over to the table.

'I always planned on doing just the one trip alongside you on the box,' he said, 'so now I'll be riding on.'

'Best of luck,' Scaggs said. 'Can't say you was of much damn help — but, hell, what can a man do when he's starin' into the muzzle of a Winchester held by one of them Geoghegans?'

'George,' Hills said, 'go get Mick a beer.'

George took a deep breath, bit off the words of protest that threatened to come flooding out, and again crossed the sawdust to the bar. Coggins was serving Tweddle. George looked sideways at the councillor, and said, 'You got any plans?'

'I've sacked you,' Tweddle said through his teeth. 'Short of running you both out of town, I guess I'm stuck.'

'You could always reinstate us. Buck can stay on as jailer, Yancey can handle the paperwork, me and Distant can do the real lawmen's work.'

Tweddle grunted, took the glass of beer from Coggins, and walked to a table well away from Hills. But there had been something in his eyes, and when George carried East's drink to the table, he was smiling.

'I've been planting ideas,' he told Hills. 'I think we can expect a call from Sid.'

'If it comes, we might have something to go on,' Hills said, 'and it also involves a feller doing some listening, and planting an idea.' He watched Mick East down half the beer in what appeared to be one long swallow, and when the guard had dragged his sleeve across his mouth he said, 'You're sure about that? It was Dewey mentioned the Geoghegans first, not the robber?'

'Damn right I did,' Scraggs said. 'Soon's I saw him, I knew. Dammit, who else is out there robbin' banks, stages — '

'And mines,' East offered.

'Yeah, mines too,' Scaggs said.

'So you saw this feller, on his horse, square across the trail and holding a rifle,' Hills said. 'Then what?'

'I yelled out, 'It's them damn Geoghegans',' Scaggs said. 'And it was, too.'

'You shouted loud enough for him to hear?'

'Loud enough for all three of 'em.'

'But two of them,' George pointed

141

out, 'were with me and Distant.'

'So he was lying,' Scaggs said, unfazed. 'Them being with you don't mean he wasn't a damn Geoghegan.'

'But he didn't say that?'

'What he said,' Scaggs growled, 'was his brothers were either side of the trail. Dammit, how many times — '

'But that could have been because when you yelled, you planted the idea,' Hills said.

'The hell it was! That black-eyed devil — '

George slammed his hands on the table and leaned forward. 'If that's right — black eyes — then he was no Geoghegan,' he said. 'I was with those Irish bandits for nigh on a week. All three of them have black hair, but their eyes are blue as summer skies.'

Mick East shook his head. 'This feller had black eyes,' he said stubbornly. 'No doubt about it — and he was a Geoghegan.'

George looked at Hills, saw the flare of excitement in the ex-marshal's eyes, the almost imperceptible shake of the head. Then, as Mick East stood up, Sid Tweddle came over to their table. East drained his glass, nodded a farewell and left the saloon. Dewey Scaggs glowered, snatched up his glass and limped over to the bar.

Tweddle sighed heavily, shook his head, sat down with his glass in his hand and looked uncertainly at Frank Hills.

'I don't know which way to turn or what to do next,' he said.

'Do nothing,' Hills said. 'Leave it to the men whose job it is to handle these problems.'

'The trouble,' Tweddle said, looking at George, 'is in knowing which men I can trust, and where the problem lies.'

'The answer usually comes,' Hills said, 'from a man laying his cards on the table.'

'All right.' Tweddle nodded. 'We've got two Geoghegans in jail, another out there in the hills with two payrolls in his saddle-bags. What happens next? Does

Jimmy Geoghegan leave his brothers to rot? Does he come in after them, guns blazing? Do I send Flint and Owen out after him before that happens — if it happens?' He took a swallow of beer, and George saw that the perspiring councillor's plump hands were shaking. 'It's like that first day all over again,' Tweddle said, looking from one to the other. 'Then, it was you two watching the bank when all the time the Geoghegans had their eyes on the mine. That doesn't exactly inspire confidence in your ability. Now there's just one Geoghegan out there, but still we don't know which way he'll turn, or what we should do for the best — and I'm stuck with Flint and Owen.'

'A lot of cards,' Hills said, 'and well spread out. Assuming they're the right ones, it's just a question of shuffling them around so we've got them in the right order.'

'They're right,' Tweddle said.

'I'd argue with that, and George would agree with me.'

Tweddle glared. 'It's clear enough. Sean and Padraig are in jail, Jimmy's free, he's got the money and he's dangerous.'

George nodded. 'Only partly true. From talking we did out on the trail, and what Dewey Scaggs let slip just a couple of minutes ago, me and Distant believe there's a joker in the pack that scatters your cards to hell and gone.'

'What do you mean, joker?'

Hills shook his head. 'Until we know for sure, it'd be wrong to say.'

'Then I'll ask Scaggs,' Tweddle said, and twisted to look across the room in time to see the whitehaired jehu's back as he left the saloon. He swore softly. 'All right, if you're not talking it seems we're back to why I came over: what do we do next?'

'I'm flattered you're asking me,' Hills said, 'but the man to talk to is Yancey Flint.'

'Protocol tells me you're right,' Tweddle said, and pushed back his chair. 'I hope to God he makes better sense than you.'

* * *

'We stay put,' Yancey Flint said.

'You tried that, and the stage was held up.'

'So we were both wrong. You and Johnson had the bank in your sights, they were out at the mine murdering Brad Forrester; me and Owen had the bank staked out, they held up the stage.'

'One of them did,' Hills said, and flicked a warning glance at George Johnson. 'Two of them had been apprehended.'

Flint shrugged, and crossed his ankles on the desk. 'One, two or all three, it was still a robbery. This time, we get it right — and that means sitting tight until Jimmy Geoghegan comes after his brothers.'

'If you talk to the Geoghegans, they'll tell you Jimmy's hide's peppered with buckshot. You think he can do it?'

'Didn't stop him getting clear when you went after him,' Buck Owen said.

'And this arguing,' Sidney Tweddle said, 'is getting us nowhere.'

The office was thick with cigar smoke. Buck Owen was standing by the safe. Flint was in his customary position in the swivel chair with his feet on the desk. George and Frank Hills had dragged straight-backed chairs close to the desk, and were watching Flint. Tweddle was standing by the open door, looking uncomfortable: on the way down the street from Clancy's he'd gone to his upstairs office, and under his fat waistline he was now wearing a gunbelt that sagged comically on the right side under the weight of an old Colt Dragoon. It was unmodified, and the percussion caps stuck out from the cylinder like warts on a hog's backside.

'Getting us somewhere,' Hills said in answer to the councillor's acid comment. 'You came to ask a question, you've got your answer: Yancey and

Buck are going to sit tight again like they did last time, wait for trouble to come calling.'

'That might be the best idea,' Tweddle said after a moment. He looked thoughtfully at Hills. 'There's just one man, as we all know. I'm sure he'll try to free his brothers, but if he's wounded there's not a lot he can do.'

'He can hightail,' George said.

'I doubt that he'll do that,' Flint said. 'His brothers are locked up, contemplating a one-way trip to the bone orchard.' He grinned at Frank Hills. 'Hell, I don't even know why I'm listening to this. As town marshal, it's my decision, and with two prisoners to watch there's only one thing to do.'

'You've got Sean and Padraig Geoghegan behind bars, Jimmy's out there with two stolen payrolls, and the Forrester Mining Company's in deep trouble. Seems to me the thing to do is swear in a posse —'

'Who needs a posse,' Flint said,

'when there's two ex-lawmen acting like vigilantes — '

'Doing your job, and doing it well,' George Johnson said.

'Then there's no more to be said,' Yancey Flint said, and looked at Sid Tweddle.

Hills scraped his chair back, stood up and looked at the sweating councillor. 'You agree with that?'

Tweddle frowned and, perhaps to hide his true thoughts and feelings, made a show of adjusting his gunbelt.

'You've told me there's something else you know,' he said at last, 'and you're refusing to share that knowledge. In the circumstances, I'm forced to go along with the appointed town marshal's decision — so, yes, I do agree. Jimmy Geoghegan will come after his brothers. When he does, he will be taken into custody and this mess will be but a memory — and, I'm sorry to have to say this, but it will be no thanks to you, or Johnson.'

But as George followed Frank Hills

out into the street and across to their horses, he again looked into Sidney Tweddle's eyes and saw in them a certain expression. This time, he thought, it was hope — and that hope had nothing at all to do with the past performance or the stated intentions of Yancey Flint and Buck Owen.

12

To George Johnson, it seemed as if his whole life for the past eight days or more had revolved around the Geoghegan Brothers. He'd shared grub with them around the camp-fire, unrolled his blankets alongside theirs, listened as their eyes twinkled in the flickering light and they concocted elaborate plans, futilely waited for them to hit Kennedy's bank when they were making their money someplace else, then gone out hunting them and damn near shot himself in the thigh and flattened one of their horses when he fell over a cliff. Now here he was again, riding out alongside Frank Hills, feeling as bone-weary as his horse — and they were hunting another Geoghegan.

Or maybe not.

He and Frank Hills had left town at a fast canter, pulling a plume of dust into the hills with the galling knowledge that Yancey Flint and Buck Owen were again admiring the light glinting on the badges pinned to their chests while sitting at ease on their backsides waiting for something to happen.

Over the likelihood of what they expected to happen actually happening, George was in two minds. Sid Tweddle had appeared to be talking a lot of sense — for once in his life — but it was hard to swallow the idea of a wounded kid risking a ride into town, saddle-bags stuffed with money from the first robbery, and using a six-gun to bust into the jail and free his brothers.

Yet the Geoghegans were a tight-knit clan, and if Jimmy Geoghegan didn't act fast he would one day pick up a local newspaper and find himself using his finger to trace the words telling how his brothers were hanged for murder.

And it was a murder committed by another man, a hard, cool customer who, so far, had made just one slip.

Hannahan's Lode fell away behind

them. They rode through the foothills with the sun a dazzling orb hitting them in the face from high above their left shoulders as it dipped towards the west. Before it got anywhere near setting, it would be on the far side of the mountains and, although they had but five miles to ride, the long shadows it cast would bring a late afternoon chill before they reached the mine.

And Frank Hills still hadn't told George exactly what they were doing.

'Ed Dyson killed Forrester, then robbed the stage, right?'

'I'd put money on it,' Hills said. 'I also believe he caught the Geoghegans at the mine with their business unfinished, and emptied the safe for himself when they hightailed.'

'You think he'll be at the mine now?'

'Why not? He's done everything right. The Geoghegans have denied murder, but they've admitted busting into the office and stealing the payroll and the one goes with the other.'

'The joke is,' George said, 'they think

Jimmy robbed the stage — and he didn't.'

'So we catch Dyson and everything gets straightened out. All the cash goes back where it belongs, the Geoghegans'll spend time in the Pen for the first robbery, but it'll be Dyson who gets his neck stretched.'

They pushed on as the sun dropped steadily through clear blue skies until its brilliant rim touched the jagged ridges of the high peaks, riding steadily along the trails snaking through the trees, and always they were alert for the sound of hoofbeats. If Jimmy Geoghegan was heading for town he would ride under cover of darkness, but Dyson had covered his tracks well and an innocent man has no need to move furtively.

When they saw the low silhouettes of the mine buildings ahead of them in the long shadows crawling across the broad hollow, George said thoughtfully, 'If Dyson's taking the woman with him, he'll go for the railroad. That means he'll head north. If they moved fast, we're already too late.'

Hills swore softly. He pushed his horse to a fast lope and cut across the perimeter of the yard, only once glancing towards the office. George, spurring after the ex-marshal, also looked that way and, as the wind flapped his hat brim, he caught a fleeting glimpse of a rider coming across the yard from the direction of the bunkhouse. Then the horsemen was lost to view and they were in the trees again. Sounds became muffled as the beat of hooves was deadened by the carpet of fallen leaves, and five minutes later Hills held up his hand. They slowed, approached Brad Forrester's house at an unthreatening, easy walk, and drew rein.

'No sign of him or the woman,' Hills said.

'What does Gerry Forrester do all day anyway?'

'From what she told us,' Hills said, 'she mooned about dreaming of what it would be like with Forrester out of her life.'

'Swapping him for Dyson ain't the world's best deal,' George said, but Hills was no longer listening. He was down out of the saddle, and with his six-gun in his hand was walking towards the gallery.

George took his time, convinced the house was empty. Yet even at that reluctant pace he caught up with Hills at the gallery steps, and the look on Hills's face tightened his stomach.

'Blood?'

George nodded, swallowing as he looked at the dried brown blotches on each of the steps; lifted his eyes and followed the ugly smear across the gallery to the front door. It was standing ajar.

'Going, or coming?'

'If someone got hurt out here, they'd be taken into the house,' Hills said.

'If there was a fight inside, whoever came off the worst would be dragged out and buried.'

Hills nodded. 'Take a look inside.'

George lifted his chin, pushed out his

lower lip. Losing his badge had made no difference to Distant. Once a lawman, always a lawman — but George had also worn a badge, so why should he . . . He squinted into Hills's cold blue eyes, nodded, drew and cocked his six-gun and went up the steps.

The door swung open silently at his touch. He stepped inside, moved a pace to his right, put his back flat against the wall. The sun had slid away from the room much earlier and left it cool. After the brightness outside, it took a moment for George's eyes to adjust. When he could see clearly, he knew the room was empty. At his feet, the bloody trail snaked across the room. It stopped at a rifle rack. A Winchester lay on the floor.

So what had happened? Had a wounded man been dragged inside, taken as far as the racked rifles — only to vanish. No. George smiled thinly in the silence. Despite the door being left ajar, the sharp bite of cordite still irritated the nostrils. A gun — pistol or rifle — had been fired in the room. Someone had taken a slug by the rifle rack, gone down, maybe in the act of grabbing a rifle to defend himself.

Or herself. Because under the faint but acrid stink of cordite, there were lingering traces of a subtle perfume.

George sighed, and went back outside. Hills was nowhere to be seen. George stepped down in front of the house, saw the scuff marks in the dirt and the traces of blood and followed the trail around the house. Thirty yards from the back wall, Hills was waist deep in a patch of scrub. The sun was beating down. A cloud of black flies hummed around Hills's head. He heard George and looked across.

'The woman?'

Hills nodded, flapped a hand at the flies.

'Makes sense. If she'd pulled the trigger, a big man like Dyson would still be in the room.'

'So where's he gone?' Hills came crackling out of the scrub, his face pale and tight with anger. 'The murdering bastard's headed north, and we're too late?'

'There's more than one way back to the mine. I thought I saw a rider just before we hit the trees.'

'Did he see you?'

'I don't know.'

Hills studied George's face. 'Why would he go back there?'

'Yeah, the safe was empty.' George shrugged. 'But he could always have put some cash back in there. Where better? Until he was ready to ride.'

'All right. Let's find out.'

They mounted up and pushed their horses back through the woods and now there was urgency in their movements for, if they were reading the signs right, the man they were hunting had killed twice. Hills again took the lead, leaning his mount into the trail on the twists and turns so that saplings were swept aside at his passing to whip back and catch George with stinging cuts as he rode close behind. In that manner they raced back to the yard. Again, Hills raised his hand. Again, both riders slowed.

The trees thinned. Across the yard the office was in shadow. A horse was ground tethered alongside the steps. Glass from the window broken as the Geoghegans made their escape still sparkled in the grass.

And then, in that same window, flame spurted. A rifle cracked, a bullet came snicking through the branches, and green leaves floated lazily down on the two watching ex-lawmen as they hastily pulled back into the trees.

13

He rode down out of the trees with the crescent moon a sliver of cold white light rising high in starlit skies, ahead of him the lanterns of Hannahan's Lode like warm sirens luring him to his death. He rode with the cool scent of night in his nostrils and one hand holding the reins high as his horse slid stiff-legged down rutted gullies or high-stepped over grassy mounds that loomed out of shadows already slick with dew, for in his other hand there was his Sharps rifle and, even this far out, he was afraid of being caught cold, afraid of what men would find in his possession.

Jimmy Geoghegan had ridden down from the Black Hills with his saddle-bags stuffed with stolen money.

If he was asked for a reason — if he was asked why, in God's name, he had not left that money stashed under rocks at the mossy bole of a tree in a place indelibly marked in his memory — he would say that if he failed in his mission the money would not matter anyway, and if he succeeded there was no saying which direction he and his brothers would be forced to take.

If he was asked why he had not stepped in, as had been planned, when Marshal Frank Hills and George Johnson came out of the darkness to take his brothers at gunpoint — or why, instead, he had not left them to their fate but gone on valiantly to hold up the stage — no answer would be forthcoming.

Jimmy Geoghegan was ashamed. In the cold dawn light he had watched from woodland no more than a hundred yards higher up the hillside as drama tore his family apart, felt sick to his stomach as the two lawmen took his brothers as easily as rounding up a couple of docile steers. He had stood numb and helpless, his mind in a whirl and his limbs frozen, his old Sharps forgotten in his hand — and had done nothing.

Now he was about to make amends, or die.

★   ★   ★

'I detected something in Sid Tweddle's tone,' Yancey Flint said, 'that suggests he's listening more to Hills and Johnson than the two upright lawmen diligently upholding the peace in this town.'

'Who?' Buck Owen said. He was in a chair near the office window, his clumsy hands trying to work some shape into his battered Stetson.

'Us, you damn fool.'

'Yeah, right.' Owen's tongue poked the gap in his front teeth as he frowned. 'I didn't hear Hills say much for Sid to chew on.'

'You weren't up at Clancy's.'

Owen stared blankly at the big marshal. 'Hell, Yancey, neither were you.'

'No, but it ain't hard to work out the bunch of them up there were doing more than buy drinks and slap each other on the back.'

Flint ground out his cigar and, in a movement about as strong and decisive as any he had made since pinning on his badge, he swung his feet off the desk and stood up.

'So what would they have been doing?' Owen said, as Flint went to the rack on the far wall and lifted out a shotgun and Winchester.

'Totting up all the mistakes we've made, and scheming over how best to get these badges off us when all this has blown over.'

'What mistakes?' Owen said, and grinned. 'Hard to make mistakes when we ain't done nothing.'

'Here,' Flint said, and tossed the Winchester to Owen. The deputy dropped his hat, caught the rifle awkwardly, then nearly dropped that as the door slammed open. Yancey Flint swung to face the cool buffet of dusty air, lifted the shotgun and thumbed back both hammers with a single wicked snap.

'Put it away,' Sid Tweddle said and, with one hand held palm-out as if to ward off the rain of buckshot, he stepped through the door with his big six-gun bumping against the jamb. 'Those prisoners secure?'

Flint tilted the shotgun, straightened to his full height, and smoothed his moustache.

'Time's pushing on. I've issued weapons, my deputy has his Winchester, I'm armed with a shotgun. It doesn't matter when or how Jimmy Geoghegan comes after his brothers, we're ready to meet every eventuality.'

'Knock it off,' Tweddle said. 'You sound like a politician.' He hitched his gunbelt, kicked the door to and looked pensively at Flint. 'Hills reckons Jimmy Geoghegan won't come.'

'Johnson reckoned the bunch of them would rob the bank — and they didn't.'

Tweddle smirked. 'And you were

convinced they'd come to town after the second payroll, but they took it when the stage was within spitting distance of Deadwood.'

'What's your point, Sid? Where's this leading?'

Tweddle took a deep breath, let it out explosively and shrugged helplessly. 'I don't know. Maybe something Hills said about a joker in the pack is getting to me.'

'What the hell does that mean?'

'I've been thinking about it. The only answer I can come up with is someone else's involved. If that's the case, then it's possible Jimmy Geoghegan won't be alone — and you and Buck could be in trouble.'

'Maybe,' Buck Owen said nervously, 'we should do like we did with the bank and put men with rifles on roofs and — '

'Yeah, and have them cursing us when they're stuck out there for hours watching nothing more than a couple of mangy stray dogs licking their privates.'

166

Flint eased the hammers down and slammed the shotgun on the desk. 'Take this, Buck, walk around town. Stay in the shadows. Keep your eyes and ears open. You see anything move that shouldn't be moving, you've got two barrels to put it right.'

'I don't think I can sleep,' Tweddle said. 'Those Geoghegans are so tricky they've got me looking under my own bed. If Buck watches the street from here to Clancy's, I'll cover the other end of town. With two of us out there I can't see Jimmy Geoghegan getting through.'

'And if he does,' Yancey Flint said, touching his ivory-handled six-guns, 'he'll have me to deal with.'

*   *   *

For Jimmy Geoghegan, the problem with being in charge of so much stolen money in his brothers' temporary absence was that he knew he'd get uneasy if he moved more than ten feet from his horse — yet the best way of getting into Hannahan's Lode without being seen was to move in on foot, through side alleys that would bring him out into the lighted main street directly opposite the jail.

How to get around this dilemma tormented Jimmy unmercifully on his way down from the hills. When, less than a mile from town, he tested the strength of his fears by dismounting and slipping into the eerie quiet of the trees to roll and smoke a last cigarette, he came out to find his horse had silently walked almost 200 yards away with reins trailing, and almost died of fright.

In the end, when the oil lamps of the town seemed close enough to touch and the heavy silence in the air told him that Clancy's had probably seen out its last bleary-eyed customer, he realized the kid who'd been praised for coming up with plans of his own had let his thinking become muddled: why leave his horse at all, when its four legs could negotiate the alleys as well as his two, and carry him away a damn sight faster if there was trouble?

He felt as if a terrible weight had slipped from his shoulders and, once released from the problem that all along had been of his own making, he covered the last mile into town with his head held high and his nose sniffing the air like a hunting wolf and began to see light when before there had been nothing but darkness.

If Clancy's was closing, the Lode's main street would be empty, the good citizens in their beds. If he was seen, it would be by the purest of accidents.

Sean and Paddy were locked in strap-steel cells. The easiest way for Hills and Johnson to guard them was the way he, Jimmy Geoghegan, was guarding the saddle-bags on the four-legged bank he was riding into town: stay with them.

And he had with him the vital element of surprise.

He was one man, and a youngster at

that. The two lawmen sitting in their warm office would not be expecting a kid who was free and rich to come storming their fortress. If luck was with him they would be complacent, maybe even sleeping.

Jimmy Geoghegan nodded, deliberately soaking up the good thoughts and shoving the strength-sapping, gut-wrenching images of blazing six-guns and helpless prisoners soaked in their own blood to the back of his mind. It was time for action, for in front of him the town loomed large and silent.

Wary now, he kneed his horse away from the inviting glow of the main thoroughfare and eased into a street that ran parallel and would bring him past the back of the livery barn to the side alley opposite the jail. He rode along a narrow lane of darkness stinking of decaying rubbish and horse droppings, automatically touching the weapons at his disposal like a soldier seeking reassurance as he advanced into battle. He had his six-gun, and the old

Sharps tucked in the boot under his right leg, but this was no night for working with the long gun. The confines of the jail meant the rifle's only use would be as a crude club, and should be sacrificed for the handgun's speed. He would go in fast, turning surprise into mind-numbing shock that would, for that instant, immobilize both lawmen and . . .

His breath hissed through his nostrils.

He had reached the alley. Faint light from the main street seeped down the narrow gap between business premises and washed over his horse's slick coat. Across the street, two men emerged from the jail in a pool of light and stood for a moment talking in low voices. On the bone-thin man's vest a badge gleamed; in his hands there was a shotgun. The other man was dark-suited and fat, but a huge six-gun hung at his hip and his hand brushed it constantly. Both men were watchful, their eyes roving restlessly and catching the light as they conversed.

Then, as Jimmy Geoghegan's horse lifted its head and the bridle tinkled softly, the fat man looked up and glanced towards the dark mouth of the alley. He took his time — seemed about to step away from the jail and start across the street. Then he shook his head, reached back to close the jail's door and they moved off in different directions.

Jimmy let his breath go and cursed softly. What the hell was going on? The thin man was not Hills or Johnson, but he was wearing a badge. Had they sworn in another deputy — maybe more than one? Was he up against three or four righteous townsfolk who'd volunteered to meet the deadly Geoghegan Brothers with a blast of withering gunfire, instead of the two bored, sleepy lawmen he'd expected?

And then, as these thoughts heaped trouble upon trouble and he gazed absently at the empty hitching pole outside the jail, Jimmy felt his stomach contract and his mind reel dizzily. He

172

leaned forwards, stiff-armed, his hands folded on the horn and his head bowed as he wallowed in the enormity of his error.

He was setting out to rescue two men, would almost certainly come piling out of the jail to make a long run for it into the Black Hills — but between them they had but the one horse. His thoughts hadn't carried him beyond the stark reality of bursting into the jail to confront the lawmen, but somewhere in the muzzy background he had always pictured Sean and Paddy's mounts dozing in front of the jail. Instead he knew that, with the two prisoners locked away and nothing left for them but the short dawn walk to the gallows, their horses would have been moved to the town's livery barn —

Which he had just passed!

'Easy, now.'

Wiping the cold sweat of fright from his face with his sleeve he whispered to his mount, quieting it as he used knees and reins to turn it about and retrace their route. It was a ride of some fifty yards. The livery barn's big rear doors were wide open, the runway dim and quiet — but where was the hostler?

As he hesitated, Jimmy recalled his one visit to Hannahan's Lode. He had ridden in late one evening when George Johnson was playing the outlaw out at the brothers' camp, and had seen an old man in the saloon. At his enquiry, Coggins had told him the man's name was Wright, he was the hostler, and he slept in a cot in the loft over the barn. Old men slept lightly, Jimmy knew, but not old men who are fond of the bottle — and on that visit he had watched Wright walk out of Clancy's and cross the street, his eyes glassy, his gait unsteady.

Even as such thoughts and their implications raced through his mind and he moved his horse into the deep gloom of the barn, he heard faint snoring from overhead and a thin smile twitched his lips. He dismounted, listening to the rustle of straw and the soft sound of horses in the stalls; saw, in the light from oil lamps and the rising moon coming in through the wide-open front doors, the sheen of worn saddles on a sturdy rail.

And then, conscious that his stupid mistake and the consequent delay were weakening his resolve and causing doubts to multiply like weeds after warm summer rain, he moved fast. His brothers' horses were in adjoining stalls, their rigs hanging together on the rail. Within five minutes, both were saddled, eyes alight and ears pricked as they lifted their heads to the night air.

Then Jimmy paused.

His original plan was now full of holes. Mounted and leading two frisky horses, his progress from the alley across the main street in the night quiet would have all the stealth of a stampede of buffalo. His only chance of getting to the jail undetected was to leave the horses in the livery barn; the quickest way there was out through the barn's big front doors.

He loose-tied all three horses to a timber upright, drew his pistol and moved up the runway. Overhead, the rhythm of old man Wright's snoring was unchanged. Straw rustled at Jimmy's passing. Cold moonlight lapped at the barn's entrance. Behind him, a horse whickered and, as he half turned, a futile finger raised to his lips, he heard footsteps.

The bone-thin man wearing the badge! When the two men outside the jail split up, he had headed towards Clancy's. Now he was coming back, and on this side of the street.

Again the horse whickered softly, and now another snorted and there was the hard rattle of hooves moving restlessly on the packed dirt runway. Outside, the footsteps faltered, then came on. Jimmy slipped into the deep shadows alongside the doors. His heart seemed to thunder in time with the footsteps. His breathing was shallow. He held the six-gun high, against his shoulder, his knuckles white on the worn grip.

Then the man was upon him, and stepping into the barn. His mouth was parted. Moonlight gleamed on gapped yellow teeth. His eyes were apprehensive, and darting. The shotgun was held high and tight in his hands.

With a grunt, Jimmy Geoghegan swung the pistol in a looping, overhand blow. The heavy six-gun slammed against the man's head. His legs buckled. As he began to go down, Jimmy hit him again, felt the jar of the second blow all the way to his shoulder. Then he grabbed the thin man's vest and, as he slumped to the ground, dragged him like a weightless sack of grain into the barn's shadows.

14

'You recall the layout of Forrester's office?'

In the hot, breathless silence under the trees overlooking the yard, the crack of the single shot still ringing in their ears yet the atmosphere deceptively peaceful, George Johnson eased his weight in the saddle and nodded.

'What do you want to know?'

'Any windows on the far side of the building?'

'No. Just the ones we can see.'

'Then Dyson's finished, he's nowhere to go.'

'But he'll fight.'

Hills smiled crookedly. 'He's got choices, the same as we have. Easiest ways are for him to walk out with his hands high, or for us to keep him in there until he starves to death.'

'Except those miners, when they

come down from the hills, they might take his side and then *we're* finished.'

'Right. No badges to justify what we're doing.'

'But there's something else about those miners.'

Hills grinned. 'Sure. Dyson'll be more scared of them, than of us. He's pulling out of here with their payroll, and although they don't know that yet, he can't wait around until they find out.'

'So, sooner or later, he's going to bust out of there.'

'You can count on it. I reckon the diggings are too far away for gunfire to carry, but he'll be itchy as a gopher on an anthill.'

Hills was silent for a moment. He eased his horse forward for a clearer view and Johnson said, 'Easy, Distant. All he needs is a clear shot . . . '

'Right now it's a stand-off,' Hills said. 'Someone's got to break it, and it might as well be us.'

'Not that way. If he plugs you, I'm

going home,' Johnson said, and Hills chuckled.

'No windows on that side,' he said, 'doesn't mean a man with a rifle can't throw a scare into him.'

Johnson grinned. 'Thin walls, if I remember right.'

'Reckon you could work your way around?'

'Spent a week with the Geoghegans, didn't I? They taught me all they know.'

'Then make use of it, George. Get up there on the hillside, without being seen. As soon as you start shooting, I'll go like hell across the yard. You see me move, come down and join the party.'

Johnson twisted in the saddle. The office was across the yard directly in front of them, and he looked away to his right through the trees at the low-slung bunkhouse. He could ride that way. There was no gap to cross. The end wall of the building abutted the timber, and beyond it the steep slopes began, littered with rock outcrops and expanses of grass. Easy. No way Dyson could see him as he cut behind the bunkhouse, and once he was above the offices there was that wall without windows. Johnson nodded his satisfaction, then turned his horse, kneed it off the trail and started through the trees.

'He's likely to come out through the door if he's carrying that payroll,' he said over his shoulder, 'but don't neglect that broken window.'

He saw Hills nod acknowledgement, then the trees were between him and the ex-marshal and he was through and working his way around the rear of the bunkhouse. As he reached the far end of the low building and started up the slope he wondered what Dyson was thinking. Feller'd probably figured he was clear, the woman dead and out of his hair, the payroll his ticket out of the wilderness. He walks into the office, picks up the sack of money — then two riders come out of the trees, he recognizes them, knows they've been to the house and must have found the woman's body.

'And now he's sweating, trying to find the guts to bust out of there before them miners come down from the hills, knowing if he does he'll face those two armed men,' George told his horse; saw its ears flick and grinned happily as he cut across a steeply sloping stretch of coarse grass to a stand of straggly trees and found himself directly above the back wall of the office.

'So if you're having trouble making your mind up, Mr Dyson,' he said softly, 'we'll do it for you,' and he slid smoothly from the saddle, drew his Winchester and jacked a shell into the breech.

As he brought the rifle to his shoulder he looked quickly down and to his left, and thought he could just see Hills's Stetson in the trees. Then he squinted along the sights and sent three fast shots into the back wall of Forrester's office. The shots were deafening in the stillness. White splinters flew from the dry wood, and from inside the office there was a startled yell.

Before the echoes of the shots had rippled away into the high timber, Frank Hills exploded from the trees. He pushed his horse across the yard at a reckless gallop, bending low in the saddle as he headed across the hump marking the centre of the hollow and straight for the office steps. At once, Johnson pouched his rifle, swung into the saddle and pointed his horse downhill. It went down stiff legged, dropping in a series of jolts that rattled Johnson's teeth and shook his hat loose. He grabbed for it with one hand, felt the horse plant a hoof that skidded off flat rock, and begin to fall sideways. Then George was grabbing for the horn as he went out of the saddle. He hit the ground hard. Breath whooshed from his body. He rolled, then slid on his back, crackling through brush stiff with thorns that tore at his clothes and skin.

Then both feet hit a flat boulder and momentum pulled him upright and facing downhill and in danger of falling flat on his face. Instead he was running, desperately forcing his shaky legs to keep pace with his toppling body. Arms windmilling, he went downhill out of control. His hat had gone. One boot heel snapped off. As it went with a pistol-like snap, he saw the door of the office burst open and Ed Dyson walk out. He came boldly, with a swagger. Under his left arm there was a sack. In his right hand, a pistol blazed.

Half-way across the yard, Frank Hills reared up, and went backwards out of the saddle. The riderless horse trotted towards the office, then came to a nervous halt.

Then George was at the bottom of the slope.

His headlong plummet brought him up against the blank wall. Suddenly, Dyson was out of his sight. George hit the wall with a bone-jarring thump, gritted his teeth as his shoulder went numb, then pushed himself off and drew his six-gun. Even as he did so, he remembered Dyson's horse, ground-tethered, patiently waiting. With a curse, he ran along the building, stumbling through the tufted grass, listening for the sound of receding hoofbeats — wondering about Frank Hills.

He burst around the end of the building. He was alongside the steps. In the middle of the yard Hills was down, motionless. Ed Dyson was heaving himself into the saddle. He'd pouched his pistol. The heavy sack was dragging him back.

'Hold it!' Johnson roared.

Dyson swung around. He saw Johnson, and snarled. The sack fell. He stabbed a hand towards his holster. Johnson snapped a fast shot, missed, stepped forward and turned his ankle on a stone. As he did so, Dyson fired. The slug took George Johnson in the knee. He felt the numbing hammer blow, felt his leg buckle and went down. On his side, gasping, he watched Dyson pluck the heavy sack from the ground. This time he made it into the saddle. He wheeled the horse, raked it with his spurs and started across the yard.

Heading north, Johnson thought. Figuring to use the railroad. And with his jaw set he lifted his six-gun and shot Dyson's horse from under him.

The killer rode the dying horse to the ground then came nimbly to his feet. The sack of money had been dragged from his hand. It was half under the horse. Warm blood was soaking into the canvas. Dyson cast a desperate glance at Hills, then bent to the gunny-sack. He grasped the tied neck with both hands and heaved. The sack held under the horse's weight, then suddenly came loose. Dyson staggered backwards, dragging it through the dust. Then, with a second calculating glance at Hills, he picked up the bloody sack and went for the downed man's horse.

Red spots were dancing behind George Johnson's eyes. From the knee down the leg of his pants was soaked with blood. He knew he should do something, but all power seemed to have seeped from his muscles. He looked blearily at Hills, saw movement, watched in a daze as the exmarshal clawed his way to his knees.

Dyson had seen nothing. His eyes were fixed on the horse, its nostrils flaring as it scented the fresh blood. It lifted its head, backed a step, then another, and Dyson said softly, hoarsely, 'Easy, boy, easy now,' and kept on walking.

But the horse's skittish movements had worked for him, placing it between him and Hills. On his knees, six-gun in his hand and with blood a terrible dark stain on his chest, Hills seemed incapable of rising to his feet and his view of the killer was blocked.

Dyson had almost reached the horse.

Desperately, George Johnson lifted his six-gun, saw the violent tremor in his aim and knew that, if he pulled the trigger, he'd miss. And then, still looking along the wavering barrel of the six-gun, his own view was blocked. For one terrifying moment he thought that the curtain of death had fallen before his eyes, and he was swamped by a wave of despair. Then he realized it was not death that had taken away his sight, but his own riderless horse: it had come down surefootedly from the steep slope where it had thrown its rider and, stirrups flapping, unnoticed, had trotted across the yard. Now it cut across Dyson's path, its muscular shoulder brushing the killer aside. The two horses who had carried Johnson and Hills over thousands of miles of mountain and plain came together, nuzzling. And, as if at a signal, they trotted away to the flatter ground where glass sparkled in the lee of the office building.

Ed Dyson was naked, exposed, a man alone in the middle of a sunbaked yard. In that yard, Frank Hills was on his knees with levelled pistol, and ten yards away George Johnson was clutching his bloody thigh with one hand while with the other he held a pistol shakily, but with indomitable spirit.

Dyson looked at Hills, at the pistol that was rock steady and lined on his chest, and wet his lips; whirled, looked at George Johnson, saw the still levelled pistol that wavered but was a constant danger — and went for his gun. But in the fall from his horse, it had been shaken loose. His hand slapped an empty holster, and his face went grey with fear as his searching gaze found the six-gun. It was lying in the dust, ten yards away. Ten yards, that might just as well have been ten miles — and his shoulders slumped.

'It's over,' Johnson called.

Dyson's lips peeled back. Something glittered in his eyes but, through vision blurred by weakness and pain, Johnson couldn't make out if it was defeat or desperation, fear, or a crazy kind of raw courage.

He had no time to decide.

Dyson spat into the dust, turned away from Johnson and Hills and, without haste, began to drag the bloody gunny-sack through the dust of the yard to where lay his six-gun.

With a single shot, Frank Hills shot him dead.

15

Inside the barn's doors, Jimmy Geoghegan stood still, listening. The unconscious deputy breathed wetly in the shadows. Otherwise, the night was still and silent.

The shotgun had hit the ground with a clatter. Breathing hard, tension tightening his muscles, Jimmy pouched his pistol, picked up the scatter-gun and stepped warily into the street. It was empty. Clancy's was in darkness. There was no sign of the second man who had headed towards the other end of town, and the jail was just fifty yards away. Lamplight gleamed in the only window. The door was shut.

Jimmy went across the street in a slanting run, slipped from moonlight to deep shadow and moved swiftly towards the jail with his left shoulder scrubbing against unpainted lumber walls. His breath rasped in his throat. A long way ahead of him down the street he thought he saw a bulky shape move and metal glint but, driven by the excitement that had gripped him in a furious rush of adrenalin as he lashed out at the deputy, his only reaction was a wolfish grin that drew his lips back from his teeth.

Then he was at the jail.

He went in without hesitation, kicking the door stiff-legged for maximum impact. The jamb splintered. The door swung and slammed back against the wall with a mighty crash. Jimmy leaped in to land spread-legged. The shotgun was cocked. In the yellow lamplight his eyes fastened on the big man slumped in a swivel chair, eyes closed, feet on the desk.

The big man's eyes snapped open.

Jimmy's savage grin was a fixed grimace, his eyes glittering.

'The keys to the cells?'

'Wha . . . '

'Keys. To the cells. Where are they?'

The big man gaped and blinked. His

hands flapped somewhere close to his fancy six-guns. Jimmy stepped forward, planted the shotgun barrel across the man's throat, plucked both ivory-handled beauties from their holsters and sent them thudding into the corner of the room. Then he stepped back and kicked the chair over sideways. The marshal hit the floor with a solid thump, face down, his feet tangled and still on the desk.

From the cells a voice sang out, 'On the wall, Young Jimmy!'

He swung the shotgun in a wide arc and swept the big man's feet off the desk.

'Stay like that, face down. Move, you're dead.'

Then he grabbed the big ring of keys from one wall peg, used the shotgun barrel to hook his brothers' gunbelts from another, and went through to the cells.

'Jesus, boy, you're a sight for sore eyes,' Sean said.

'If you ask me,' Padraig said, 'the

193

youngster looks a mite frazzled.'

'Wouldn't you, if you were running around robbing stage-coaches and rescuing incompetent bandits who would be better off behind a plough?'

Padraig chuckled as the key grated and his cell door swung open. 'Well now, that's something I'd like to have seen, Young Jimmy out on the trail with his six-gun pointed at the guard's middle and that grizzled jehu up on his box — '

'I didn't do it,' Jimmy said, unlocking Sean's cell. 'I was skulking in the woods, turned and ran like a dog with its tail between its legs.'

Padraig had lifted his gunbelt from the shotgun and was buckling it around his hips. Now he paused, and frowned. 'Somebody did it. The stage came in without the money, that fat feller crossed the street expecting Hills to have the payroll and then blew his top when he heard — '

'Never mind that now,' Sean said. 'Jimmy, have you got the money we know we lifted?'

'With the horses.'

'Where?'

'In the barn.'

'And who's out there in the office?'

'I was about to ask you. He's a big feller wearing a marshal's badge, but it's not Hills.'

'Hills was thrown out, along with our good friend George.'

'So where are they?'

Sean grinned. 'Out looking for you, I shouldn't wonder.'

Padraig chuckled. 'Ah, Jimmy's the clever one, he's got them all running around like chickens looking for their heads.' To Jimmy, he said, 'If that feller out there is able to walk, bring him in and we'll give him a private room.'

Yancey Flint could walk, but when Jimmy brought him through his legs were noticeably shaking. When the cell door clanged shut behind him and he realized his fate was a cage, not a bullet, they almost buckled with relief.

'Right, then,' Sean said, 'if one of you

gentlemen will lead the way we'll go pick up our mounts.'

'I think I cracked a deputy's skull,' Jimmy said. 'I left him in the barn.'

'Goodness me, yet more surprises,' Padraig said. 'Is there anything else you've not told us, Young Jimmy?'

'Another feller's out on the street keeping his eyes open. A fat man with an enormous pistol.'

'Sid Tweddle,' Sean said. 'He's carrying a percussion Dragoon, and we'll not worry too much about him.'

Nevertheless, they did leave the jail with supreme caution, Sean stepping out first to flatten against the wall, and only calling the others out when he was certain the street was clear.

'Where did you see this Tweddle?'

'That way — I think,' Jimmy said, pointing to his left.

'Then it's lucky for us the barn is in the other direction,' Padraig said.

And now it was Jimmy who led the way, again hugging the lumber walls as he ran towards Clancy's then cut across the moonlit street and in through the livery barn's big doors.

Sean and Padraig were behind him, breathless. Jimmy nodded towards the shadows where a pair of booted feet poked out into a shaft of moonlight, then swiftly went down the runway to the horses. His first act was to pat the saddle-bags he had brought down from the hills, feel their comforting bulk. His second was to toss the shotgun into the straw and fling himself into the saddle.

In an instant, all three Geoghegan Brothers had mounted and were swinging the horses towards the rear door where moonlight was cut by the high buildings and the back street was in darkness.

Yet even as they pulled their horses' heads around, Jimmy sensed that something was wrong and, as he looked about him in sudden panic, a voice rang out from the doors behind them, quavering but insistent.

'Throw down your guns!'

'Goddamn, it's Tweddle!' Sean said.

'And the law,' another unsteady voice chipped in, and the bone-thin deputy Jimmy had mercilessly beaten to the ground with his six-gun stepped out of a stall close to the back street, blood streaking his face, straw clinging to his stockinged feet.

'They've tricked us, but to hell with the both of them!' Padraig roared.

'Ride, lads!' screamed Sean.

Spurs raked the flanks of horses eager for flight. Each one leaped forward, eyes rolling white in the darkness, lips curled back from flashing teeth in which metal bits glittered. But as the brothers acted with fearsome speed, so too did their opponents. A stunning boom made the air tremble; the slug from Sid Tweddle's big Dragoon Colt slammed like a driven log into Jimmy's horse and it went down in a quivering heap.

Then Buck Owen bent to pluck the discarded shotgun from the packed dirt, and let loose with both barrels.

The double blast as he snatched at both triggers drove the horses wild.

Strands of straw rained down from the loft. The thunderous roar and the brilliant flash drew a terrified yell from the old hostler. Suddenly, every man there was staring into red-misted blindness. When it cleared, Padraig Geoghegan was reeling in the saddle, his shoulder a bloody mess. Sean, hanging on to his rearing horse, snapped a fast shot that knocked Owen back into the stall. The Dragoon roared for a second time. Sean's Stetson went flying.

'Here, Young Jimmy!' Sean cried, and brought his horse back onto four feet and stretched out a bent arm.

'The saddle-bags!'

'For God's sake, leave them, man!'

'No — !'

His protest died on Jimmy's lips as Sean drove his horse at him and hooked him off the ground. Padraig was already leaving the barn, slumped and rocking in the saddle. Sean followed, riding with one hand gripping the slack reins, Jimmy half carried, half running, face twisted with fear until at last he swung high enough to throw a leg over the cantle as another shot from Tweddle's Dragoon split the air and the doors and peppered them with needle-sharp splinters.

And then nothing could be heard but the rasp of harsh breathing, the hiss of racing pulses in ears ringing from the sound of gunfire in the big barn, the rapid tattoo of beating hooves as the Geoghegan Brothers — bloodied and empty handed — rode out of Hannahan's Lode.

16

'Riders coming,' Hills said.

'If it's a posse,' George Johnson said, 'I'll eat your hat and mine.'

'And you're so tight up against me you could to do just that.'

The two ex-lawmen were riding double, George on the cantle behind Hills, his leg a stiff log bound with a bandanna and as painful as an aching tooth. Over Hills's shoulder the lights of Hannahan's Lode shimmered before his weary gaze. From the saddle horn a taut rope led to Johnson's horse. Aboard it, Ed Dyson was face down, wrists and ankles lashed beneath the horse's belly. And as, from time to time, Johnson had found cause to hang on during the agonizing ride from the mine, his hands had pressed into the crispness of blood drying on Hills's shirt and he knew that his cheerful and laconic friend was in poor shape.

The riders came towards them at a gallop, dark shapes outlined against the lamplit town.

'Two,' Hills said. 'Tell me, George, can you think of two men who would be riding fast from town at this time?'

George chuckled weakly. 'We brought them in, Yancey Flint couldn't hold them. I'd say it's the Geoghegans.'

'Do we stop them?'

But there was no need or time for George to reply. As the distance between them rapidly closed, the riders fleeing the town saw the horsemen ahead of them on the moonlit trail and veered suddenly. They came flashing past through the short grass, pulling a thin plume of dust, the glint of weapons in upraised fists.

Then came recognition.

'Away home to bed, George,' Sean Geoghegan sang out gaily. 'We've got wounds to lick, so you can rest awhile.'

'And the money?' Frank Hills yelled.

'Alas,' Sean cried, 'we left it all

202

behind us with those two stupid fellows trying to — '

His words were lost in the thunder of receding hooves, becoming a thin distorted sound that yet carried with it — to George's ears — the reckless, noble spirit of the man whose food he had eaten under the stars, the brothers who had tormented him yet not once threatened him with harm. Could he apply that definition — a worthy one, indeed — to lawless bandits? Was there, lying in wait for him in Hannahan's Lode, the terrible consequences of their black side — for surely escape even from fools such as Yancey Flint and Buck Owen would result in some bloodshed . . .

'Two of them were riding double,' Frank Hills said.

'Been trouble all around then,' George said. 'But who's come out on top?'

'Let's wait and see,' Hills said, and they did that, remaining silent as they rode through the Geoghegans' dust for the few hundred yards that brought them into the Lode and down the main street to the jail where, once again, they dismounted with a prisoner.

But this one needed no strap-steel cell. They left Ed Dyson's body on the horse tied to the hitch rail, Frank Hills making his way shakily into the office with his left arm clamped to his wound, George Johnson limping behind him with a face like chalk, teeth clamped against the pain, and the bloody gunny-sack of Brad Forrester's money he was dragging threatening to pull him off balance.

Inside, a man sat in the swivel chair with his feet on the desk alongside a big Dragoon pistol, and the sight brought to Frank Hills's face a tight and disbelieving grin.

'What the hell are you doing here, Sid?'

'If I was spiteful, I could say I was doing your job — but as I relieved you of that position, I guess I'll have to say I'm standing in for Yancey Flint.'

He looked at Johnson, at the bloodstained pants, the bloody sack, and nodded. 'I guess that's all of it. I got what the Geoghegans took from the mine, you got . . . ' He frowned. 'Who *did* rob the stage?'

'Ed Dyson, Forrester's foreman. He surprised the Geoghegans when they were robbing Forrester, shot his boss when they'd gone, took the money they left behind and went on to rob the stage and get his hands on the replacement payroll. I guess he and Gerry Forrester fell out. We found her body behind the house.'

'Jesus! Did you get him?'

'He's outside, waiting for the hearse.'

Tweddle sighed. 'Looks like I was wrong from the start. You and George were out of a job but did all the hard work, those two fools — '

'Tweddle!'

The roar came from out back, and Hills raised his eyebrows.

'Flint,' Tweddle said. 'The Geoghegans inflicted some punishment. Buck

Owen is dead, Yancey Flint's suffering the ignominity — '

'The what?' George said.

'Mortification,' said Tweddle.

'Shame,' Hills said, and George nodded as he saw the light.

'He's suffering the shame of being locked in one of his own cells,' Tweddle finished. 'What do you want, Flint?' he roared.

'I'm marshal of this town, I want out of this goddamn cell!'

'Not any more, you're not. Throw out your badge, Flint, and I'll appeal to George's good nature.'

For a long moment there was silence. Then, from out back, there came a faint tinkle.

Tweddle grinned. 'I've already told you Buck's in no shape to hold on to his badge or his job, and I guess what we just heard was the sound of Yancey Flint handing in his resignation. George, as deputy marshal I'm sure you know where the keys are. Go release the man, and bring me Frank's badge.'

206